Meet the employees of
Deadly Force, Inc.

Luke Simpson: Founder and president. Vietnam Vet, ex-cop, former CIA, he got tired of playing by the rules. Now, this deadly soldier of fortune picks the jobs—and calls the shots.

Jake O'Bannion: Management and services. This hard-nosed ex-New York City cop is the caretaker of Deadly Force's HQ on Superstition Mountain. And his fighting skills are more than lethal.

Ben Sanchez: Warrior-for-hire. He fought with the Rangers in Nam. Now, this silent Apache is a part-time mercenary—and one of the deadliest on Simpson's team.

Tran Cao: Science and technology. Toughened by the war in his homeland, this sharp-witted South Vietnamese can master the world's most advanced computers—and most devastating weapons.

Calvin Steeples: Chief pilot. He was a flier in Nam. Now, he's a cropduster—when he's not helping Simpson destroy more dangerous vermin.

Deadly Force

The DEADLY FORCE Series
Published by Berkley Books

DEADLY FORCE

Crime Wave

Mark Dixon

B

BERKLEY BOOKS, NEW YORK

This is a work of fiction. The characters, incidents, places and dialogues are products of the author's imagination and are not to be construed as real. The author's use of names of actual persons, living or dead, is incidental to the purposes of the plot and is not intended to change the entirely fictional character of the work.

DEADLY FORCE: CRIME WAVE

A Berkley Book/published by arrangement with
the author

PRINTING HISTORY
Berkley edition/August 1988

ISBN: 0-425-10977-1

A BERKLEY BOOK® TM 757,375
Berkley Books are published by The Berkley Publishing Group,
200 Madison Avenue, New York, NY 10016.
The name "BERKLEY" and the "B" logo
are trademarks belonging to Berkley Publishing Corporation.

PRINTED IN THE UNITED STATES OF AMERICA

10 9 8 7 6 5 4 3 2 1

Chapter 1

The old man knew he was in trouble. Whitey was after his ass.

He had left Morton's Corner Grocery at nine-thirty on this hot Chicago morning with a grocery bag parked on one skinny arm, his head bowed to the bleary morning sun that shone above the roofs of the tenement houses, intending to make his way to his apartment on 156th Street without bothering anybody or being bothered by anybody. At his age, just making the four-block trip to Morton's was pain in the ass enough without having to worry about some street punk hoisting his wallet or knocking him around, and crime had been rising like a rocket lately, so he generally made this journey early in the morning while the punks were sleeping.

But these guys, these guys tailing him, they weren't punks.

He looked back over his shoulder once again to make sure his cataract-ridden eyeballs hadn't fooled him. No such luck. Two middle-aged white dudes in their best Sunday suits, each carrying a briefcase and looking as

serious as an undertaker, were ten yards behind him and
dogging his trail. He had veered across the street at the
corner of 153rd and Walnut, and they had followed him.
He had jaywalked back to this side of the street half a
block ago, and they had followed him. They weren't
closing the distance, but they weren't dropping back, either. They were wearing sunglasses and had on hats. Not
many white dudes wore hats these days.

The old black man, Henry Lutes by name, quickened
his pace. His spindly bowlegs ached with arthritis, and his
heart, no spring chicken anymore, was beginning to thump
painfully in his bony chest. The grocery bag was getting
heavy, and he shifted it to the other arm, getting a faceful
of celery in his nervousness. He spit out leaves and glanced
back again. What could these dudes want? They looked
like undertakers, all right, or G-men out of an old Edward
G. Robinson movie, or tax men, or . . .

Tax men. Of course. They were the IRS, and they were
after Henry Lutes for a little crime he had committed long
ago, 1937 or so. During the Depression a twenty-year-old
Henry had been out of work and on the verge of starva-
tion, and down in Florida he had picked oranges with the
migrants for two weeks one hot summer, and the grove
owner had paid him cash money without taking out deduc-
tions or any of that legal finery. That had to be it. The IRS
computers had finally worked their way backward far enough
to catch him. Now they would want to be paid, delinquent
taxes plus penalty, and Jesus Christ in heaven, that would
be fifty years' worth of interest.

Henry felt himself go a little weak at the thought of all
those decimal points and dollar signs but pulled his cour-
age together and urged his feet to move faster. This was
the South Side of Chicago, no-man's-land for a man with a
fancy suit and a briefcase, and it wouldn't be long before
the gangs who ran this territory came out on the streets to

greet a new day. When they saw these dudes in their hundred-dollar hats with James Bond sunglasses perched on their white noses, they would go apeshit, literally apeshit on them. The tax men, if they survived, would soon give up on the idea of collecting from Henry Lutes.

Only, that didn't happen. The streets were quiet on this Tuesday morning. Things had been pretty rowdy lately, lots of gang violence, lots of fires, lots of news coverage. The South Side seemed to be taking a breather today, as if it had been smoldering under the weight of crime and decay too long and needed one morning, this morning, to cool off. There was nobody on the sidewalks but little kids playing in the dirty puddles left by the previous night's rain, some women, and an occasional old man intent, like Henry Lutes, on his own survival.

Henry came to the intersection of 155th and Hickory Streets and stopped. Cars ambled past, thickening the sultry air with the smell of exhaust. He chanced a look back. The two men had stopped, too, still ten yards behind. They were staring at him. Sunlight flashed on their glasses.

One of them, the shorter and fatter of the two, had sweat trickling down his white face. He looked fidgety. The other dude was tall and cool. He would be the Head Man, Henry decided. James Bond, himself. In his briefcase would be ten pounds of legal documents, each bearing the name Henry Lutes and instructions to pack him off to prison if he didn't pay. Well, by God, Henry Lutes wouldn't pay. He had earned that picking money honestly, and come to think of it, had there even *been* an income tax in 1937? Or had he picked those oranges in 1940? He looked back to the street, frowning, bewildered. Who the hell had been president the year he'd picked those oranges?

He walked across the street. His knees ached and his

neck was sweaty. The grocery bag was too heavy, and he switched it back to the other arm. Inside, he had a carton of eggs, a whole fryer chicken, bacon, a Hormel canned ham, soda crackers, a bag of apples, two loaves of bread, some celery, a can of Vienna sausage, and a Snickers bar. In the evenings he watched *Mr. Ed* reruns and ate a can of Vienna sausages with crackers, howling with laughter at the crazy things that horse would do. Before he took his teeth out, he would eat the Snickers bar, and then he would go to bed. It was a familiar routine. Everything in the life of seventy-eight-year-old Henry Lutes was pretty familiar, and had been since his wife, Evvie, had died. Except this routine, this being dogged by James Bond and his fat sidekick on a hazy July morning in his own neighborhood.

A car honked; somebody shouted something nasty at him, something about being old and skinny and a blind asshole. He ignored it, ignored everything but the street passing beneath his feet and the possibility that the IRS might cut his welfare, cancel his food stamps, garnish his meager retirement checks, and send him to prison. All this would only happen if they caught him. If only he could make it to the safety of his apartment, get inside, lock his door, hide under the bed, cover his ears, and close his eyes, then he would be safe. The inside of his apartment was his world, his domain. The bastards would have a search warrant before they set foot inside it. Henry Lutes might be scared, but he was no fool. A search warrant would give him time to think, time to explain himself. He had been a young man in the Depression. He'd had no schooling. He didn't know about taxes.

He made it to 156th, his own street, before he stopped at the curb and looked back again. James Bond and Sweatboy were still there, Sweatboy looking even soggier, James dashingly cool. They pretended to inspect the sky.

Henry hated them suddenly, hated them worse than he hated his old age and his arthritis. He hated them for scaring him like this. He hated them for ruining an otherwise nice morning.

His anger built up like hot steam. They weren't looking. He snarled at them. He squinted his eyes and made faces. He stuck out his tongue. He took his celery out and shook it at them.

"Go away," he hissed, but it was to himself, too quiet to be heard by anyone but himself. They were government boys, and they could put you in a world of hurt. You don't mess with the Man.

They stopped gazing at the sky and looked over to him. Guiltily he put his celery back, turned, and walked. This was 156th, his own turf. He had lived here since 1954. He and Evvie had raised kids here, one of them now an Army officer who sent an allotment check every month. Henry smiled to himself. His confidence began to come back. He was kind of a hotshot here, somebody the people looked up to. He was the guy who got on the landlord's ass to fix things. He was the guy who, four years back, formed an impromptu tenants' union when the landlord tried bully tactics to collect his rent. He was the guy who told the landlord to his face that he was a cheap, cocksucking vampire when the landlord last raised the rent. And now, with crime going berserk and everyone so afraid for their lives that they wanted to move away, it was Henry who still walked to Morton's Grocery to show them it could be done.

He made it to the front steps of his building and paused, looking up. Three steps up and you were in the shadowed entranceway facing a pitted old steel door painted green. From there you entered a hallway that angled left to a stairwell. You took the creaking, foot-eroded wooden steps that led to the second floor. You came up to a grimy,

yellowed window covered with broken steel mesh. This
was the first landing. You went left and went up more
stairs. You smelled the familiar odor of dust and wood rot,
you caught the sour aroma of neglected baby diapers and
marijuana smoked by kids the night before. You came to
the top of the stairs, out of breath and hurting at the knees,
and took the hallway left again to the fifth door on the
right, you took out your keys and opened four locks, you
stepped inside, and you were safe.

But first, Henry thought, looking at the green steel door
and its imagined safety, you tell these dudes the facts.

"You need a warrant," he shouted, taking one step up
and turning. He put his groceries on the step above and
straightened again. His knees ached like bad teeth, but it
was the ache of victory, the kind of ache a tired runner has
after crossing the finish line. For the first time in years
Henry enjoyed it. He had beaten these dudes in a race to
his house.

"I won't say a word till I see a warrant," he crowed.

The two men, who had stopped at their usual position of
ten yards behind, looked up at him. The cool one smiled.
The sweaty one wiped his face. The cool one stepped
closer.

"I know my rights" Henry shouted. "I've watched
TV!"

Now they both came at him. Henry wondered briefly if
a warrant applied only to one's actual apartment, or to the
whole building. It was a legal question he decided to leave
to the Supreme Court. As they moved toward him, he
snatched up his groceries and hurried inside. By the time
the green door had banged shut, he was already halfway
up the first stairwell. The door banged again, and he
realized they had come in; a moment later he heard them
thudding up the stairs behind him, stepping mechanically,
without haste and without regard to the Supreme Court.

He made it to the first landing with his breath already rasping up and down in his throat. He had smoked unfiltered Camels for fifty-four years, and his lungs, like his heart, were no spring chickens anymore. He grabbed at the banister with his free hand, hauling himself up two steps at a time, passing through dusty bars of sunlight cast through the first-landing window. His grocery bag bounced on his arm. The celery tumbled out and thumped down the steps. Trip on that, he thought wildly, and then was consumed with worry that his eggs might break from all this running.

Second landing. He went left, weaving down the hallway, stumping drunkenly on his bowlegs while fumbling in the pocket of his baggy old-man's trousers for his keys. He did a hopping little dance on one foot, aware that the men had reached the second floor, too, and were thudding down the hallway. He managed to get his keys out and tried to make sense out of them in the dim light that filtered from the window at the end of the hall. He held them close to his face, breathing hard on them. It was hot up here, hot enough to make you squint. The smell of dead wood and old, dusty carpets was thick and choking. And these keys were practically identical, dammit, and having cataracts as thick as plate glass didn't help. Henry jammed a key into one of the locks, turned it, and found that it clicked open.

James Bond and Sweatboy stalked him as he hurled the door open and ran inside. Henry slammed the door shut on them. He groped for the light switch, scrabbled at it, forgetting if it flipped up or down. It went up with a click, and his front room was full of light. He dropped the groceries on the floor and began turning locks, grinning, finally cackling to himself when they had all clicked into place.

"*Warrant!*" he screamed gleefully. Sweat streamed down his face. "*You got to have a warrant!*"

The voice on the other side of the door was soft but firm. "Mr. Lutes?"

"Ask your computer," Henry screamed. He dropped to his knees to look through the keyhole below the knob. He saw, dimly, legs. "Ask your computer who I am!"

There was a moment of hesitation. "We have a warrant," the soft voice said.

Henry pulled back. His face screwed up in consternation. He scratched his wiry white hair. "Show me," he said finally.

"Open the door, then."

"Through the keyhole." Henry put his eye to it. "Show me through the keyhole."

He heard latches click; they were opening a briefcase. He saw something white that was pressed to the keyhole.

"Here's your warrant, Mr. Lutes."

He scratched his head again. By God, it was white, and it looked like paper. He thought of all the TV cop shows he had ever seen. People were always demanding a warrant, but when the cops produced one, who ever saw it? They were white, and they were paper. What the hell was a warrant supposed to look like, really?

His heart sank. They had him. For picking oranges in 1937, or 1940, whenever it had been. They had him computerized.

"Just a second," he said. He stood and turned the locks.

They came in, brushing past him. Sweatboy was sticking the white thing back in his briefcase. They turned and faced him.

"Shut the door," the tall one said.

Henry shut it. This was private business, this lynching by paper. The government boys were concerned for his privacy.

"I swear, I didn't do it," Henry said.

James Bond removed his sunglasses and placed them on

the table by the door where Henry generally put his keys. He placed his briefcase on the floor, snapped the latches, and withdrew a wad of cotton and a bottle. He opened the bottle and shook some of the liquid out on the cotton. He closed the bottle. He put it back. He stood up. A very neat man, Henry thought dazedly. He also thought that for IRS men, this was very strange behavior. What was this business with the bottle?

"Hold him," the neat man said to his sweaty partner.

Henry was grabbed from behind. His elbows were pinned together. His shoulders popped, shafting pain along his arms. With the pain came the swift realization that these were not government men at all, that the whole business about the IRS and back taxes was a figment of his overactive mind, and that he was in very deep trouble that had nothing to do with picking oranges.

He opened his mouth to scream. The wad of cotton was mashed against it and his nose. He smelled funny stuff, chemicals or medicine. He refused to breathe. He was hit in the stomach, and breathe he did.

In three seconds he dropped to the floor.

"Fucking amazing," the fat man said.

"Hold him up," his partner said.

The fat man hoisted him easily and pressed him to the door.

"His arm," the man Henry had thought looked like James Bond said. He opened the second briefcase and withdrew a hammer and four sixteen-penny nails. He went to Henry, positioned his gnarled black hand at the upper right corner of the door, and drove a nail through it into the wood.

"Other arm," he said.

The fat man raised the other one. James Bond nailed Henry's other hand to the door.

"Spread his feet," he said. "Tiptoe."

Henry's right foot was held. James Bond drove a nail through his black old-man's shoe. Blood seeped up around the nail and dripped off the toe of his shoe. His other foot was nailed. Henry hung there like a sack.

"Get the sign. Hurry."

The fat man got the thing Henry had mistaken for a warrant. It was a four-inch by six-inch placard on a string. He hung it around Henry's neck. In neatly typed letters on it were the words GET OUT NOW.

They stood back and looked at him.

"Think he'll hold?"

"He'll hold till they peel him off."

They collected their briefcases. Henry moaned, and his dangling head jerked.

"Go," James Bond said. "It wears off quick."

They left, closing the door, now very heavy on its hinges, behind them. They were out on the street, half a block away, when Henry woke up and began to scream.

A thousand miles away, at a dusty spot on the map known as Higgery, Arizona, a man named Vergil Ketchum was swatting flies.

There were hordes of them this time of year, late July in the desert, and God himself couldn't know how the critters managed to breed and feed when there was nothing around for miles but sand and saguaro cactus. And they were big, too, practically horseflies. Vergil was suspicious of every fly in the two-hundred-square-mile area he called home, for here they could feast on the melting candy bars in the display case by the cash register, breed in the stinking outhouse Vergil called a rest room, and dive-bomb Vergil to pass the time. How he hated them, the goddamn flies.

"Here's one for *you*!" he roared, swinging his flyswatter. He was sitting in a high-backed rocking chair by the gumball machine, keeping one eye on the dusty stretch of

Route 17 out front for customers, the other eye on the bugs. Two summers ago a California tourist passing through from a trip to Texas had given him a Texas flyswatter, which was three times the size of the ordinary ones, and he had grown fond of it, the way most men grow fond of a faithful dog. Customers didn't come by too often this time of year—or any other time of year, for that matter—and if the truth be known, Vergil was going a bit batty from all the solitude. If it weren't for the flies to keep him company he would go insane.

Today he would get some company he hadn't reckoned on.

Around eleven-fifteen a battered-looking Chrysler Le Baron, bright blue under its coating of dust, pulled in beside the pump, and a man got out, leaving the motor running. Vergil noticed nothing unusual in this, except that the man looked wrinkled and bedraggled and generally dead on his feet. Even through the foggy glass storefront Vergil could see the big purple pouches under his eyes and the stubble of whiskers on his cheeks. He was wearing a white shirt with the cuffs rolled back, and dark slacks. Salesman, Vergil decided. There was somebody else in the car, he noticed while the door was open. A little girl was asleep on the seat.

Vergil sat back and swatted flies. Folks passing through here usually worked the knots out of their legs for a minute, used the pisser, checked their maps, and wondered just where in the fuck they were. Folks stayed to chat because the desert waited out there, dry and vast and unnerving. Vergil saw no need to hurry for this fella.

The man squinted down the highway. He checked both ways for an unusually long time. He finally eased the car door shut and came inside, jangling the bell over the door.

Vergil got up and laid his swatter aside. "How do?" he said. "Hot one, huh?"

"Fill it up," the man said, digging out his wallet. He seemed weary but somehow nervous. He kept looking back to his car. "Unleaded."

"S'all I got. How's your water?"

"Fine. Look, just make it ten bucks, okay? That's all I've got left."

"Ten bucks it is." Vergil eyed him. Fidgety guy, maybe no salesman at all. "What line of work you in, mister? I like to think I can tell by a man's look. You sell insurance?"

"Sure," the man said. "Insurance. The gas, please."

"Where do you hail from? Phoenix?"

"Sure. Come on, will you? My daughter's roasting in the car.

"What's your name?"

"Vandevere. Larry Vandevere. The gas?"

Vergil ambled to the door, thinking of nasty divorces and the way some guys will snatch their own kids. That's what this looked like, maybe. "Where's the missus today?" he asked. "Staying home?"

"Sure. Hurry up, okay?"

"You're the boss." Vergil opened the door, no longer giving a shit who this guy was or what he was up to, when he saw a big black Lincoln roar up beside the Chrysler in a wash of road dust. Two men leapt out.

"Shit," the nervous fellow breathed. The color was gone from his face.

"Busy day," Vergil remarked, and suddenly he was being shoved aside as the man named Vandevere pushed past him and flung the door fully open. The bell tinkled shrilly. Vandevere sprinted to his car and was jerking the door open when the two men from the Lincoln came around and grabbed him. One of the men hit him in the mouth.

Vergil gaped at them. "Well, hell," he said.

Vandevere appeared to be involved in a fight for his

life. One man had gotten an arm around Vandevere's neck from behind and was twisting his head back and forth. The other man was dodging his kicking feet, lunging in and out to land a few punches to his gut. Dust floated up around their legs. The pump hose got kicked free of the pump, thumped against the car, and sagged to the ground, dribbling gas.

The little girl popped up in the window, wide-eyed and sleepy. She saw what was happening and screamed.

Vergil Ketchum blanched. Suddenly there was a riot underway on his front stoop. Nothing like this had ever happened before. He stepped back, tripped over his own feet, and fell into his rocker. He sat bolt upright and reached for the only weapon his mind, in its alarm, could think of at the moment. He reached for his Texas flyswatter.

"*Stop it!*" he roared, diving for the door. He hauled it open and screamed at them. "*Not on my property, you don't!*"

Things went on regardless. Vandevere had reached back and gotten two handfuls of hair from the man strangling him and was trying to flip him over. The other guy pounded his gut mercilessly. Vergil charged out into the bright morning sunshine, waving his flyswatter. The little girl screamed and screamed.

"You men get *outa* here!" Vergil cried. He came up to them and began swatting in a frenzy. The man hitting Vandevere in the stomach got smacked full in the face and staggered back, pawing at his eyes. Vergil hit him again, on the chest, on the shoulder, on the elbow, driving him back. Then he turned his attention to the man strangling Vandevere.

"Stop that," he screeched, hauling back to bring the wrath of Texas down across this man's face. That was when the other man, aware now that he had been hit with an oversize flyswatter and nothing more, swung out and punched Vergil hard in his sizable belly.

"*Whoof*," Vergil said, and his legs folded underneath him. He sat down in the dust, making faces.

"Hold him tight, goddammit," one of them said. They picked Vandevere up, writhing and twisting, and carried him to the rear of their car. The trunk was opened and Vandevere pushed inside.

"The girl?"

"Better get her too."

One of them went back. Vergil tried to stand, but his breath was still frozen in his lungs, his belly full of stone. He watched as the man reached to open the Le Baron's door.

The little girl squawked, turned her face to the windshield, scrunched down, and jammed on the gas. The Le Baron bellowed, fishtailing forward, shooting dust in fountains from the rear wheels. She made it out to the road, and the tires squealed on the hot asphalt. She headed south down the road like a drunk.

"Ah, shit," the man said. He turned back, started to run, then stopped and looked down at Vergil. He grinned at him. "Here's for your flyswatter, you cocksucker," he said, and picked up the hose. He aimed the nozzle at Vergil and squeezed it. Lukewarm gas gushed out, splashing in his eyes, drenching his clothes.

"Now for a match," the man said. "Where, oh, where, is a match?"

Vergil got up, blubbering and gasping. He got up faster than he had gotten up in years. Vergil found his feet and ran, frozen breath and belly full of stone forgotten, wringing wet and stinking like a refinery. The man's laughter chased him. Vergil ran across the cactus-strewn desert as fast as he had ever run in his life.

Chapter 2

Luke Simpson and Jake O'Bannion were playing mind games. No one was winning.

They were sitting on the redwood deck of the simple A-frame cabin that was Deadly Force Incorporated's modest headquarters, hunched over a patio table, protected from the morning sun by a large white umbrella that thrust up from the center of the table on a pole. The patio furniture—four white metal chairs, the white metal table, and the umbrella—was brand-new, something Jake had picked up on his last trip to Phoenix. How he had packed the stuff on the gyrocopter (the umbrella stood nine feet tall no matter which way you laid it) was something Luke had decided he would never ask. The crusty ex-NYC cop was always full of surprises.

"Concentrate," Jake said. His green Irish eyes were full of seriousness. "You can do it."

"Right," Luke said. He frowned and grunted, bent over the table staring at a swizzle stick perched on a glass. Beneath his crew cut was a lean and angular face, screwed up now with false concentration. A hint of a smile hung on the corners of his mouth.

"Harder," Jake said.

They had had a leisurely breakfast on the new patio table, and the dishes were now pushed to the side. On the rim of Luke's juice glass Jake had balanced a swizzle stick from the previous evening's nightcap. Luke was supposed to move it with mental force alone. Jake had stayed up late to watch Letterman on TV, and some mystic had performed this stunt. Alpha waves, or some such. With such a super IQ, Jake figured it would be no problem for Luke.

Luke squinted and moaned. The swizzle stick, a red plastic one Jake had appropriated from a bar in Phoenix, swayed a little.

"It moved," Jake said. His paunchy face, full of middle-age wrinkles, spread wide with awe. "You did it."

"The power of the mind," Luke said, and screwed a finger at his temple. "Salami, salami, baloney. The wind did it, Jake. Only the wind."

Jake stuck a finger in his mouth and held it up. "Not a breath of air, man." He waved an arm to indicate the broad panorama of desert that surrounded the cabin, and the extinct volcanic cones of the Superstition Mountains that rose in the distance like jagged teeth. "You have the power to control all this, my friend. You have the power to move mountains bigger than those. All you need is practice."

"All I need is better lungs. I blew on the swizzle stick, Jake. That's how I moved it."

"Bullshit. You didn't move your mouth."

"I farted, then."

Jake laughed. "Bullshit again. A guy like you, you can do things, things other men can't. Hell, look what's sitting right under our feet. A hundred thousand square feet of artificial caverns and caves you designed yourself, enough guns to equip an army, airplanes, helicopters, tanks and rockets and bazookas—"

"LAWs," Luke said, interrupting.

"Fucking LAWs, mortars, mines, enough computers to fill a barn . . ."

"One computer. My Cray."

"One computer, then, and a big motherfucker at that. Jeez, you've got everything down there, and you know why?"

"I'm game. Why?"

Jake grinned. "Because you've got mind power. A lot of other guys just sit around dreaming, saying, 'Someday I'll do this and I'll do that,' but you, hell, you made it *real*. You had a dream and you made it real. That takes more mind power than moving a goddamn swizzle stick around does."

Luke leaned over and laid a hand on the beefy man's shoulder. "Why, Jake, you talk just like the president of my fan club."

Jake jerked back, reddening visibly. "Don't go getting the big-head on me." He passed a hand through his curly red hair, pausing to massage his bald spot thoughtfully. "I'm trying to make a point here, dammit, and the point is this: I think—you decided to go out on your own and do it better than anyone else. You were in Vietnam and you saw how it worked. You were a cop and you saw how it worked. You were CIA and you saw how it worked. You saw all the wrong ways it was being done and knew how to do it the right way. Any other guy would have just swallowed it down and put in his thirty years, set his sights on retirement, and to hell with everybody else. Only, you didn't."

Luke frowned, beginning to have a vague and uncomfortable idea of what O'Bannion was leading up to.

"You told everybody else to just fuck off, and went out on your own. You had an idea, and you made it reality. Not many guys would have the guts to do that."

"Guys like who, Jake?" He prodded his old friend on the shoulder, then punched him playfully. "Is this breast-beating time, Jake? A little early in the morning for that, isn't it? Don't you Irish always wait till about midnight and get drunk for this? Poor Jake O'Bannion, he put in his thirty years even though he knew how fouled up the system was. Next you'll be telling me about your poor sainted mother, how she whiled away her golden years in Ireland. And your Uncle Paddy, may God rest his soul."

"Ah, you," Jake said, smiling again. "Can't you let a guy feel sorry for himself?"

"Only if he's got something to feel sorry for. Christ, man, you were a New York City cop. That's the toughest beat in the world. I admire the hell out of any man who can walk that beat and survive three decades."

"Kickbacks," Jake said. "Bribes, payoffs, crooked lawyers, asshole judges. It made me sick the first week after I strapped on my nightstick and knew what the real scoop was. I could have just told them to go to hell."

"Like I did?"

"Like you did."

"Then you're forgetting something."

"What?"

"I had six million bucks in my hand when I gave them the finger. It made it a lot easier."

"Yeah." Jake settled more comfortably in his chair. "Your hotshot invention. Must've been some deal, to make you that much money."

"A simple patrol car computer tie-in," Luke said, and tapped his forehead. "Mind power, man. Mind power." He aimed his blue eyes at the swizzle stick. "I command you to *fall*!"

The red plastic stick wobbled on the rim of the glass— and fell.

Jake O'Bannion gazed at him mildly. "That time *I* farted."

They were laughing together, enjoying the shade of the new umbrella and the beauty of the red-brown desert with its decoration of green cactus, when motion off to the left caught Luke's eye. He sat up straighter. On the narrow ribbon of asphalt that led past the cabin to wind across the desert floor toward Higgery, the only paved road within thirty miles of this area, a car was approaching, no more than a glint of sunlight from this distance, but a badly driven glint. It was weaving all over the road. And there was another car behind it, right on its tail.

Jake saw him stare. "Kids," he said. "Drag racing."

"I don't think so."

They watched the cars. In half a minute they were close enough to identify a blue sedan and a black, larger car. The blue car was swerving wildly, at times charging up onto the shoulder in a billow of dust. Distantly the noise of squealing tires drifted on the thin desert air, followed by a heavy, metallic clunk as the two cars collided. They separated again, the blue car veering hard off the road. It spun sideways, obscured by dust and spraying sand.

The black car screeched to a stop. It was thrown into reverse, and roared backward, throwing blue smoke from its tires. It stopped, and two men jumped out. They ran to the other car.

"Looks like somebody's mighty pissed," Jake remarked.

Luke stood up, frowning. "I want a closer look." He went into the cabin and returned carrying a pair of binoculars. He set them to his eyes. The cars were still about two miles away, but the powerful Zeiss lenses brought them in sharp and clear. The dust around the blue car was settling. Luke could see the rear tires spinning uselessly in the sand, digging themselves in. There didn't appear to be a driver. Luke blinked, straining to see.

The two men from the black car hustled over to the blue one. One of them yanked the door open, lunged inside, and came out dragging a little girl. She writhed and kicked. For a moment her face was in clear focus, bright under the sunlight. She looked vaguely familiar.

Then Luke saw the man swing out and hit her with his open hand.

"Damn," he muttered. He set the binoculars on the table, aware that Jake was looking at him questioningly. Something bad was going down out there, practically in his front yard, something bad that ought to be stopped. You didn't have to be a cop to see that.

Luke glanced over to the Chevy 4×4 sitting in the driveway. It would take two, maybe three minutes to get out there in that. His eyes snapped over to the trusty two-seater Bensen gyrocopter Jake kept parked on the airstrip that ran through the middle of the Deadly Force compound. It was strapped down against the sometimes violent desert wind and would take too long to get airborne. Whatever was going to help that kid would have to get there fast.

"You still keep that varmint rifle of yours in the cabin?" he asked Jake.

Jake nodded. "Sure, but it's only a little .222 Hornet."

"Get it."

Jake jumped up and ran into the house. "She's only good for a couple hundred meters," he said when he came out. He handed the rifle over. "You'd be lucky to hit a barn at this distance."

Luke pushed his chair aside and knelt by the table. With the barrel of the rifle he pushed dishes aside to clear a space. "Always aim high," he said. He rested the rifle on the table and pressed his cheek to the stock. "How are the sights?"

"Zeroed in two weeks ago, but for my eye, not yours."

"Good enough. Spot for me."

Jake snatched the binoculars up. "Go."

Luke snapped the safety off and brought the sights to bear on the black car's windshield, then aimed high, absurdly high, thankful that it was a windless morning. He cracked off an exploratory shot.

"Nothing," Jake said after a second. "Man, that little kid's fighting like a tiger."

He put the sights on the windshield again, then raised them up, higher this time. He squeezed the trigger. The little rifle popped like a firecracker. "Some glass ought to bust," he said.

"Not this time. They've heard us, though. They're looking around."

"Hmm." He sighted in on the windshield again, then went up, higher, until blue sky stood in front of the sight post. If this didn't work, he would start from scratch, working his way left and right. He squeezed the trigger and the rifle bucked.

A pause. Then: "Bingo, Luke. Lower left quadrant. Try high and to the right."

"What're they doing?"

"One guy's staring at us. The other one's got his hands full with the kid."

Luke sighted in on the staring man, who was separated from his busy partner by about eight yards, no more than a dot in the rifle's sight. He sighted high and to the right. He pulled the trigger.

"Oh, man," Jake said, chuckling. "He just got stung by a bee."

"Where?"

"His right shoulder, it looks like. Yeah, I see blood now. You've messed up his white shirt."

"Do I have a clean shot at the other guy?"

"Hell, no. Wait . . . the girl's broken away. The guy's

holding his face, like maybe she clawed his eyes. She's running to the black car . . . she's going around back . . . I can't see what she's doing.'' He hesitated, then lowered the binoculars, frowning. ''Looks like she's pounding on the trunk. What kind of lunatics have we got over there?''

''Beats me.'' Luke sighted in on the tiny stick figure that was the second man, who stood just behind and to the left of the blue car, levered the barrel upward, and fired. Jake put the glasses to his eyes.

''I think you parted his hair, Luke. He's holding his head and running around in circles. Yeah, I see blood on his face now. He's hollering at the other guy. Now both of them are heading back to their car.''

''And the little girl?''

Jake was silent for a moment, watching. He reached up and scratched his bald spot. ''Okay, the black car's taking off. They got the message and are leaving the little kid alone. Only she's chasing *them* now. She's running down the road after them.''

Luke laid the rifle down. ''Let's go see what she's got to say.''

They sprinted for the 4×4. It took, as Luke had estimated, nearly three minutes to get there, and Luke had it floored all the way. The big-wheeled Chevy bounced and bucked over the twisting road.

When they came upon the little girl, she was on her knees in the middle of the road, bent over sobbing into her hands, a portrait of absolute misery. Luke stopped the truck a good distance away and clambered down, wondering if perhaps he hadn't interfered in haste. The little girl seemed to be crying because she'd been left behind. Then why had she fought so hard?

He walked up to her with Jake beside him. She had short blond hair and was wearing a plain blue dress with a square white collar, the kind of dress, Luke thought, that a kid might have to wear at a strict private school. She had on black patent-leather shoes and white knee-length socks, one of which had slipped down and was bunched around her ankle.

As Luke and Jake's shadows fell across her vision, she gasped and looked up. Luke saw terror in her red-rimmed blue eyes. He also saw a face that he had seen before.

"Missy?" he said, going down on his knees beside her. It had been nearly five years and she had changed a lot, but it had to be her. In the cast of her eyes and the line of her jaw he could recognize Larry Vandevere, an old friend from his days on the San Perplejo PD. Larry had taken a job with the Chicago PD at about the same time Luke told the SPPD to go to hell and went to work for the CIA. That had been right after Larry's wife was knifed to death in their neat suburban home one night by an avenging dope dealer. So what the hell was his daughter, older and bigger than when Luke had bounced her on his knee at Larry's house so many years ago, doing out here in the middle of the Arizona desert?

"Missy? It's Luke Simpson. Do you remember me?"

She stood up. Sweat had pasted her bangs to her forehead. Her face was flushed pink from the heat. There was an angry red handprint across her cheek. She rocked on her feet. "Luke?" she said. "Luke?"

"Yeah, babe." Luke took her hands. "Where's your daddy, honey? What's going on?"

"The car," she blurted. She began to cry again. "He's in the car."

Jake ran over to the blue Chrysler, which had dug itself into the sand to the axle and was still running. He bent inside, turned it off, and turned back to Luke. He shrugged.

Luke pulled her close and patted her on the back, feeling sheepish and awkward. "He's not there, honey."

This brought a fresh round of tears. "No," she cried,

pulling away from Luke and pointing down the road. She stamped her feet. "The *other* car! They put him in the trunk!"

Luke stood up. Jake trotted over, shaking his head. "They've got a good head start, Luke. And once they hit Higgery, there's five different ways they can go."

"Who are they, Missy?" Luke asked. "Who were those men?"

"I don't know," she wailed. "Daddy said we had to keep running. He said we have to find Luke. He said we have to find Deadly Force."

Luke and Jake exchanged glances. "You found us, honey," Luke said grimly, and pulled her toward the 4 × 4.

Jake had the nylon straps off the gyrocopter two minutes after they got back. He set the choke on the little two-cylinder Tecumseh engine, stood behind it, and gave the propeller a spin. Blue smoke farted out the side muffler. It backfired like a gunshot. Cursing, he leaned over again and gave the propeller another huge counterclockwise push. It spun jerkily, then smoothed into a blur, the engine blatting.

The Bensen was his favorite toy of all the toys available at DFI, but keeping the cranky Tecumseh in running order was an almost daily chore. Fortunately he had worked the thing over just yesterday, installed new plugs and plug wires, and it seemed to be running alright. He had no desire to fall out of the sky in this contraption. He plopped himself in the right-hand seat and buckled up.

"No time for anything better," Luke said, and handed him the varmint rifle. The little girl, Missy, clung to his hand.

"Yeah," Jake growled. He put the rifle across his thighs and dug in his back pocket. "A zillion bucks worth of arms down below, and I get this. From now on I plug coyotes with an Uzi.'' He produced a silver flask half full of brandy, unscrewed the cap, and took a short swig. "One for my stomach, boss."

Luke slapped his shoulder. "Bring her dad back, Jake. I know you can do it." He stepped back and gave the overhead rotor a spin.

Jake put his flask back and levered the throttle. The gyrocopter surged forward, the rotor picking up speed in the growing wind, becoming a blur at the top of his vision. The engine howled and rattled. Thirty yards across the dusty, red-brown runway, the copter hoisted itself suddenly into the air, leaving Jake's stomach behind as it always seemed to. He squirmed in his seat, swallowing and grimacing, remembering that morning's eggs and bacon with unusual clarity. The feeling passed quickly, and he concentrated on following the road.

As he swooped over the abandoned blue car, it occurred to him that it had been a strange sight, seeing Luke kneeling in the middle of the road like that with his arms around the girl, patting her back with such an expression of bewildered helplessness on his face.

Jake O'Bannion had known Luke thirteen years now and had never seen him on his knees for anybody. If Luke had a soft side, he had kept it pretty well hidden up to now. It had been this hardness, this unyielding, go-getter attitude that had made Jake so dislike Luke when he first met him that winter of 1975, when Luke came to New York on vacation.

It was the idea of a fancy-pants California rookie cop taking a vacation in the dead of winter that had seemed so funny at first, and then so irritating to Jake. Jake had been at his 111th Precinct desk wading through paperwork in triplicate when the lean, young Luke Simpson had breezed in, dusting the snow off his shoulders, flashing his San Perplejo badge and asking to see the cop with the highest kill record in the precinct. The desk sergeant, old Cyrus MacKenzie, had escorted the twenty-four-year-old hotshot to Jake's desk, barely hiding a smile. "This young feller wants to see you," he had said. "He's on vacation from California. Says he wants to observe our operation. Young feller, meet Jake O'Bannion."

Summer never ends in California, Jake had thought. And this guy's probably never seen snow before. Not to mention a dead body.

"How'd you happen to find the 111th?" Jake asked, cocking his jaw toward the wooden chair beside the desk. Luke sat down, stiff as a ramrod, his youthful face stony and set. Steel poker up his ass, Jake thought wearily.

"I hear it's the toughest," Luke replied.

"They're all tough in New York."

Luke leaned toward him. "How long have you been on the force?"

"Twenty-seven years come March. How about *you*?"

"Two years, one month, six days."

"Fancy that."

Luke looked around. "Pretty shoddy quarters. Where's the lockup?"

"In the basement. It's shoddy, too, but we're thinking of redecorating."

"What kind of side arm do you carry?"

Jake opened his jacket. "Chief's Special five-shot. And my undershirt is from Bloomingdale's."

"What about long arms?"

"Daisy BB repeater." Jake sighed. "Look, son, I've got a shitpile of paper to do here. What's the point?"

"I'm thinking of moving to New York. San Perplejo's too dull."

Jake nodded. "I think I get it. You're tired of helping old hippies across the street and getting cats down out of palm trees. You want to be where the action is. You want to be useful. You want to kill bad guys.''

Luke's cool blue eyes didn't flinch. ''I want to use my talents where they'll be most effective.''

Jake leaned back in his squeaking old chair and folded his hands over his potbelly, tired of this. ''Take my advice, son,'' he said. ''Stay the hell in Saint Purple, or whatever it is. We don't need your type in this city.''

That conversation had taken place on February 16, 1975. Two days later Jake found out just how badly New York City needed Luke's type.

It was a hostage situation, the nastiest kind: family member gone berserk. The husband of the family, cooped up with his wife and eight kids in a two-room tenement, out of work, out of dope, out of sanity, began tossing the kids out the third-story window. Detective O'Bannion was the second officer on the scene. The first lay wounded on the sidewalk in a light dusting of snow, shot through the top of the head as he tried to go inside the building. Two of the kids had already been tossed, one of them, a baby, remarkably far away; it had smashed through the windshield of a car parked on the other side of the street.

Jake and his partner called for backup. They talked with the husband via bullhorn. Between shots, and over the warbling, screaming voice of his terrified wife, he told his demands: the voices in his head had to stop tormenting him. When the kids were dead, they would. That simple.

To prove his point, he dropped a shrieking toddler out the window.

Jake called for SWAT.

A crowd began to gather. More patrol cars arrived, sirens blasting. Policemen huddled behind their cars while shots and screams rang out. The wounded cop on the sidewalk moaned.

Everything waited on hold for SWAT to arrive. The last

thing on Jake's mind was the cocksure young cop from California, though he'd had a feeling the guy was still hanging around, doing the observing he'd told old Mac-Kenzie about. It wasn't until he saw Luke on the roof that he thought about him at all, and then it came to him with terrible sureness that the young cop was about to get himself killed.

He had taken his shoes and socks off and begun crawling down the side of the four-story building, using the cracks between the bricks for toe- and fingerholds. He was, as a voice in the crowd that ringed the scene shouted out gleefully, Spiderman. He inched downward while the crowd gasped and pointed. The berserk man saw this, leaned out, and started shooting upward. Luke made himself flatter. Sparks jumped off the wall beside him.

Jake opened fire. Glass shattered and rained down on the street. The man jerked back inside. The wife screamed and screamed.

Luke started crawling again.

"Fucking idiot," Jake moaned, but his opinion of California cops was inflating rapidly. When the insane man poked his head out again, the entire force opened fire, driving him back.

Luke made his way down, stopped beside the window, swung a leg out, and hauled himself in.

The cops charged the building. But it wasn't necessary at all.

A few seconds later the insane man sailed out the window. No one would ever know that his neck was broken long before he hit the ground.

Luke spent some time in the 111th's shoddy lockup, but Jake made sure none of the charges—interfering with police officers in the line of duty, criminal recklessness, and homicide—ever found their way to paper. When he let Luke out, Jake told him never to set foot in New York again, but if he did, give him a call and they'd share a drink together.

That call finally came in 1982, the year Jake retired. They shared that drink, and Luke told him about Arizona and what his new money had built under the desert there in the heart of the Superstition Mountains.

"Bullshit," Jake said. "I gotta see it to believe it."

He came. He saw.

Deadly Force Incorporated. A dream made real by the toughest man Jake had ever known. But a man soft enough to go down on his knees and hold a frightened little girl in his arms, looking a little frightened and confused himself.

"The big puss," Jake said now, grinning as he guided the gyrocopter along at a crisp eighty-five, its top speed. Higgery was coming into view, an assembly of houses and stores and crisscrossing streets on the sun-bleached desert floor. Highway 17 intersected with Interstate 10 here, which fed north into Phoenix. Four country roads met here, too, but Jake doubted if the men would have bothered with them. Both sporting gunshot wounds, doubtless superficial considering the distance from which they had been shot, they would probably hightail it all the way to Phoenix before stopping to lick their wounds. From there they could disappear in any direction they wanted to. And that poor bastard roasting in the trunk—he must be having a hell of a good time. Surely they'd stop once in a while to let him get some air, if they wanted him alive.

But that depended, of course, on just who *they* were.

Jake hefted the rifle in his free hand and popped the magazine out. Six shiny brass cartridges were nestled inside. He shrugged noncommittally and shoved it back in. Six ought to do. Maybe the men weren't even armed.

"Piece of cake," he said aloud, buzzing over Higgery and veering north to follow the interstate.

That's when he spotted the car.

CHAPTER 3

There was a lot more of Larry Vandevere in Missy than just a shared resemblance, Luke discovered. She was one tough nine-year-old.

She'd been barely four when her mother was killed. The murderer, a skinny, bearded hippie named Cosgrove, had had a longstanding grudge against Patrolman Vandevere, who had busted him more times than either could count. Cosgrove, a small-timer, spent his days in and out of jail, usually hanging around San Perplejo East Side Elementary trying to peddle grass to the kids when he was free. He was one of those dope merchants too small really to bust hard, too big simply to ignore, and too goddamn obnoxious to pass by without busting in the face. Fed up with the court's namby-pamby handling of the Cosgrove matter, Larry Vandevere, with Sergeant Luke Simpson's tacit approval, had taken it upon himself to beat the living shit out of the man, in order to convince him to peddle his wares in some other town.

When Cosgrove held Judi Vandevere down on her own bed one balmy afternoon and vengefully slit her throat with a rusty buck knife, he looked like he had slipped and fallen headfirst into a meat grinder.

Missy had hid herself under a bed during Cosgrove's mad rampage through the house. When Larry came home from work four hours later and found his house destroyed and his wife dead, Missy was standing at the foot of the bed calmly running her hand through her dead mother's hair. She had put two aspirin in her dead mouth to make her better. She was able to explain calmly what had happened. She was able to identify Cosgrove. She was able to testify at the trial. She never broke down.

And now that Jake was on his way and Luke and her were in the house fixing a couple of Cokes, she was that cool, rational little kid once again.

"It was two days ago," she said, accepting the tall glass from Luke and sipping at it briefly. She was sitting at the kitchen counter with her patent-leather shoes hooked over the top rung of the stool, her dress neatly smoothed over her knees. She set the glass down and looked at Luke with her cool blue eyes that were so much like Larry's. "Daddy came home from the department early. He picked me up at summer school. He was real upset. He had been upset all week, but Tuesday was the worst. He got a suitcase out of the closet at home and packed it, real fast. He said we have to move quick if we're going to keep moving at all. He said we were going to visit Aunt Margaret in San Perplejo, but I knew he was just saying that to keep me from getting scared. Later he told me about you and Deadly Force. He said we had to find you before they found us."

She cocked her head quizzically. "Luke, aren't you going to call the police?"

Luke shook his head. "We don't have a plate number off the car, honey. And if your daddy wanted the police involved in this, he wouldn't have been looking for me.

The police and I don't get along too well. He knows that. Besides, Jake is right on their tail. He can do things the police can't.''

She seemed to accept it. ''They caught up to us once before—in Kansas, I think. It was the middle of the night. Daddy was so tired from driving he had to stop. They jumped us in the rest area. Daddy knocked one of them out and locked the other man in the trunk. He flattened their tires and threw their keys in the weeds. But he said they'd hot-wire it soon enough.''

Luke frowned. ''He didn't try to shoot them?''

''He doesn't have a gun. When he picked me up that day, his holster was empty. Besides, I think he knows them. He called one of them Rudy. I asked him who they were, and he said they were rats.'' She smiled thinly. ''One of them is named Rudy Rat.''

''No gun, huh?'' Luke thought back to his last days as a policeman in California, when the new chief, an ultra-liberal milksop, had personally lifted Luke's own side arm from its Bianchi Sidekick holster and deposited it in a drawer. Had things in Chicago come to that?

''What kind of cases was your dad working on then?'' he asked. ''Do you know?''

She shook her head. ''He won't involve me in his work. Not after what happened to Mommy. But one evening he was watching the news while I made supper, and he started hollering at the TV. He was so mad, he couldn't eat.''

Luke's eyebrows lifted questioningly. Larry had always been a bit of a hothead, but to shout at your own television set? ''What was the news about?''

''I don't know.'' She smiled again. ''I like cartoons better.''

''Sure you do.'' Luke lifted his glass and drank. The golden hands of the huge deadwood clock on the south wall, one of Jake's projects to while away the hours between missions, showed eleven forty-five. Jake ought to be closing in now. Pretty soon they would have some answers.

"Have you had breakfast yet?" he asked. "We could cook till Jake gets back with your dad. That is, if you like to cook."

"I do," she said. "But I really couldn't eat."

"When's the last time you had a meal?"

She shrugged. "I had a Hostess cupcake at a gas station last night."

"Then I've got just the thing." He turned to the refrigerator and swung it open. "Bacon and eggs for Missy, cooked any way she likes them. If she does the cooking, that is." He laughed. "I have to make a phone call. The skillet's on the stove."

"Okay." She got up. "I'll make some for Daddy too."

"Sure." Luke went into the living room and picked up the phone. He dialed the information number for area code 312, and got the Chicago metropolitan PD number. He dialed it and was immediately put on hold.

"Bureaucratic assholes," he muttered under his breath.

A short time later the phone clicked, and a female voice came on. "Police."

"Give me Personnel, please."

He went on hold again. Tunelessly he whistled an old Doors song while waiting. The phone hissed and crackled in his ear. It clicked; a man this time.

"Personnel."

"Yes, could you tell me the status of Sergeant Larry Vandevere?"

"What do you mean?"

"I mean, what is his status?"

"Who's calling?"

"Mayor's office. His Honor got a ticket, and we want this guy's ass."

"Oh. Okay. Hold on."

Click. Luke waited. He whistled. Through the big picture window in the west wall the desert scene stood like a mural painting, where saguaro marched rank on rank to the purple spires of the Superstitions. The sun burned down on a glorious day. He wondered how long Larry had been in that trunk.

Click. "Okay, got his file. What do you need to know?"

"What's he doing giving Mayor Washington a goddamn ticket, that's what. Is City Hall his usual beat?"

"Actually, no. Sergeant Vandevere is assigned to the South Side. He was, at least. He's recently been reassigned to the Jackson Park area."

"Is that where he is now?"

"Lemme see. Yes, that's where he is."

"Still on duty?"

"Yes indeed."

"At this moment?"

"There's no flag on his file, so he's definitely on duty. Will His Honor want to see the officer in person for a reprimand?"

"Fuck, no." Luke hung up. His own PD didn't know he'd been missing since Tuesday. That was odd. If a cop in a tough town like Chicago turns up missing, you automatically assume the worst. Apparently nobody there even gave a shit. He went back into the kitchen and put on a false smile for Missy. "How's it coming?"

She turned and smiled at him sprightly. Bacon sizzled in the skillet, filling the room with its smoky aroma. "Okay. Daddy likes his eggs cooked soft, so it won't take long. Think they'll still be hot when he gets here?"

"I hope so, honey."

*   *   *

Jake followed the black Lincoln for several minutes, letting his reduced speed drop his altitude. They were tooling along at a good clip, but not fast enough to get them stopped by the local law. Jake guessed sixty-five as he dropped down beside them—and shot through the back window on the driver's side.

The driver looked over, his eyes and mouth three dark *O*'s. A bright trickle of blood was oozing down his face. Luke had indeed parted his hair, and a bit of his scalp. The other fellow had a flower of blood on his shoulder. Neither one looked very happy.

The Lincoln slowed. Jake was in the passing lane, the copter's three wheels a foot off the road. The wind blasting against his face seemed hotter this close to the ground, somehow denser. Telephone poles whooshed past. No cars were coming.

He dropped back, keeping pace, and fired again, puncturing the glass behind the driver's head. The man ducked instinctively. The Lincoln swerved and the tires barked. It swung over onto the shoulder, fishtailing.

Jake hauled the joystick back, gave throttle, and swooped skyward with his stomach groaning.

"Urg," he moaned, straining forward against the G-forces. "Goddamn flying golf cart." He pushed the rifle to his lap as he swung the craft in a tight circle and dug his flask out. The brandy was hot and burning, but it mellowed his stomach. He smacked his lips and put it away, grimacing, then grinning. Damn fine stuff. His queasy guts were tamed.

The Lincoln had found the road again. Jake flew overhead, leveling out, leaned over, and shot down through the roof.

A small silvery hole appeared in the black paint. He could almost smell the panic coming from the car. They were sitting ducks.

A car zipped by in the other lane, the occupants looking up, gawking at Jake. They honked. Jake waved. He leveled off beside the Lincoln as soon as they had passed, and aimed the rifle at the driver's face. He made pull-over motions with his head.

The window rolled down. The man in the passenger's seat bent down, then reappeared again. He leaned over across the seat and levered a shotgun out the window.

"Holy shit," Jake said.

Orange fire jetted out the shotgun's black barrel just as Jake pulled back on the joystick. The copter was as quick as a hummingbird—but not quick enough.

A hot sledgehammer of buckshot tore into Jake's right leg, slamming it sideways into the joystick. The Bensen wobbled in a sudden leftward dive. The telephone poles beside the road blurred closer.

Jake grabbed for the stick and yanked it back to center. It was wet with his own splattered blood, greasy in his hands. He jerked it back and zoomed skyward with no thought at all for his stomach, no thought at all for anything but getting out of this new and deadly line of fire.

The motor began to chatter unsteadily. The copter hesitated in its ascent.

"Oh, hell," Jake breathed.

Buckshot clanged against the sheet-metal underbelly of the gyrocopter, knocking it sideward in the sky. The motor chugged and popped. Jake glanced down, seeing the road, and the desert, and the black car rising up to meet him with a shotgun sticking out the window. He thumbed the throttle up and down. The Tecumseh burped. It rattled like an overworked power mower.

"Aw, *please*!"

He was falling back, losing ground to the Lincoln. The shotgun's dark bore followed him. He saw orange fire, heard the blast, and reflexively drew himself together.

Steel shot hammered beneath him. Some of it hit the spinning rotor with a high, discordant twang.

The motor fired, died, fired again. He reached back and worked the choke, knowing it was useless. You do not choke a hot engine.

Unless, of course, you are falling out of the sky and are out of choices.

He knew the copter would autorotate to a fairly decent landing; that wasn't the problem. The problem was these Bozos and their shotgun. What if they decided to stop and have a quick little firefight? Bullets were in short supply here.

The Tecumseh roared alive, faltered, roared. Jake guessed buckshot wounds to the gas line, or an incomplete cut through a sparkplug wire. He pulled the joystick farther back to slow his descent. His leg felt warm and painless. Wetness trickled into his shoe. He fumbled with the hot motor, burning his hand on the cooling fins, searing his knuckles on the muffler. He found a thick wire and traced it with his fingers, his face bunched up with concentration, his red eyebrows a single line below his forehead, the tip of his tongue poking out between his bared teeth.

The Lincoln was slowing. The man with the shotgun fired again. The copter jerked. A pellet seared across Jake's cheek like the tip of a hot match and pinged off the copter's frame behind his head.

A fiery glint came to Jake's green Irish eyes. He let go of the joystick and swung the rifle to aim at the car, remembering at the last moment not to shoot up the trunk. He popped off four rounds and was satisfied to see the rear window crumple in on itself, a nest of cracks.

The Lincoln speeded up.

Jake found another wire and followed it with his fingers. The motor revved and slowed, revved and slowed. He was hit with a sudden machine-gun burst of electricity that flashed from his fingertips to his toes. He jerked back, nodding. Cut plug wire, nothing more. He held the wire together and the motor smoothed instantly. He rose in the sky like a bird freed from a cage.

The Lincoln was pulling ahead. Bent like a contortionist in this uncomfortable position, Jake steered down low enough to read its license plate, memorized it briefly, and veered off to the right. He estimated he had one bullet left, an engine that needed immediate attention, and a leg that was leaking blood into his shoe like a fountain. Even a guy like Luke Simpson would see the futility in further chase.

There were other ways to handle a matter like this, better ways.

He headed home.

That afternoon a crippled woman was set afire in her Chicago living room.

Her name was Ellie Parker. She walked with the aid of two canes. She lived in a tenement home one block from where an aging black man named Henry Lutes had been nailed to his apartment door. She had heard the wail of an ambulance's siren that morning but had ignored it, as she ignored most of the sounds of the city. Had she craned to look out her window, she might have seen Henry trundled out of his building on a stretcher by two medics. Had she looked hard, she might have noticed that police cars were conspicuously absent from the scene. But she didn't look because she was involved in her own problems.

Bobby Ewing had been shot three times in the back of the head. J. R. was involved in a dirty deal that might cost him Ewing Oil. Sue Ellen was back on the bottle. Cliff Barnes was in jail for assault. And Miss Ellie, poor gentle Miss Ellie, wasn't sure if she should go ahead and marry Clayton, or wait for Jock to come back from the dead.

Ellie Parker loved *Dallas*. She loved all the reruns

WGN showed in the daytime. She particularly liked Miss Ellie, the matron of South Fork, because they had the same name, and because Ellie Parker knew that if she had been born rich and white with two good legs, she would have *been* Miss Ellie, instead of a diseased old woman surviving on welfare and food stamps in a vicious slum. She would have been *genteel*.

She heard noises and bangings drifting up from the floors below. She heard muffled screams. She heard feet running up the stairs. She ignored them.

Somebody shuffled outside her door. Ellie Parker looked up from the TV as her front door split down the middle with a brittle snap. A crowbar smashed the wood apart, and a hand reached through to undo the locks.

Ellie screamed.

They came in, three young men wearing Levi's jackets with the logo of the DeathMasters gang emblazoned in fluorescent orange across the backs. They were sweating on this muggy afternoon. They kicked Ellie's TV over on its side. They smashed a lamp. They knocked the pictures of Ellie's grandchildren off the walls. They worked with furious intensity, destroying her apartment. When they were done, they turned on Ellie.

One of them produced a can of lighter fluid. He squirted her with it. She screamed and squirmed. Blindly she swung her canes. Another produced a lighter.

She burned to death in her chair. The fire department arrived ten minutes after flames were seen licking out her window, and other windows in the decaying brownstone building. An ambulance arrived with them. The WGN Action Cam stood by and filmed.

The police never showed up at all.

The phone rang as Missy was coaxing the eggs and bacon out of the skillet onto plates. Luke went into

the living room and fetched it up on the fourth ring.
"DFI."

"Deadly Force Incorporated?"

"That's right."

"Mr. Simpson, please."

"This is Simpson."

"Long-distance from Washington. Hold, please."

Click.

Luke smiled bitterly, tempted to slam the phone down.
A call from Washington meant urgent business. This was a
damn poor time to be getting a call from the feds, but
that's just the way things worked in that screwed-up city.
Better this, though, than to have some second-ranked bu-
reaucrat coptering in with a sudden life-or-death mission
and a bunch of papers to sign. At least on the phone it was
easier to put people off, easier to say no. This business
with Larry had first priority over anything the CIA had to
offer.

"Mr. Simpson?"

"In person."

"Our representative will be touching down at your location very shortly."

"Oh, swell. Do you guys ever knock first?"

The voice was smug. "Consider yourself knocked,
Simpson."

The line went dead as Luke took in a breath to reply. He
looked at the phone in his hand, chagrined. He suspected
the rank-and-file guys at the Agency didn't care for him;
this pretty well confirmed it. They knew he was a maver-
ick, one of their own who backed out of the Company
straitjacket and struck out for freedom and profit on his
own. They probably placed him little higher than dogshit
on their list of favorite things. But when they needed
something done, something they either couldn't handle or

wouldn't handle, who the hell did they call? Dogshit himself, of course.

He put the phone back together and went into the kitchen. Missy had the two breakfast plates on the counter and was sitting patiently. Her eyes were wide and bright as she looked out the kitchen window.

"Getting too warm?" Luke asked. "I can turn on the air."

She shook her head. Steam wafted off the plates, drifting up through the streaks of sunlight that slanted through the window. Luke felt his heart go out to her. Her father was all she had left. He reached out hesitantly and put his hand on her arm. What could he say to a girl who had been through what she'd just been through? Chin up? Don't worry? Hang in there, baby? What?

"How do you like Arizona?"

She shrugged. Her eyes searched the sky through the window.

"Probably not so well, so far."

"It's all right."

"The weather's nice today." He mentally chided himself, amazed at his own inanity. What could he say to comfort her? That her daddy and him had been the best of friends, that Patrolman Vandevere had probably lost his wife, her mother, because Sergeant Simpson had secretly okayed the off-duty beating of the sleazy dope peddler named Cosgrove? Who could have foreseen the crazy thing that would follow?

"I see something," Missy said.

Luke looked. A dark speck hung in the bright blue sky outside the window, too big to be Jake's little Bensen. It was the CIA chopper, drawing close.

"It's a helicopter," Luke said. "Some business I have to attend to. Stay here, okay? I'll be right back."

He went out the door into the sunshine. The chopper

arrowed toward the compound, hovered for a moment, and dropped down on the runway. Sand puffed in flat clouds around it. The noisy Bell turbine wound down, and Luke walked across the deck, pausing at the railing to see who would come out.

The side door swung open. A man in a suit stepped out. He shouted something to the pilot and shut the door. Luke was sure he had never seen him before. He walked toward the cabin with his clothes rippling under the copter's muted wind.

Luke went down to meet him. Under normal circumstances he would be less than happy to see anyone from the CIA. He had too many memories of the Company, too many bad feelings to ever forget the way they had scuttled him off to a desk when field operations was his natural calling. Under normal circumstances he would be less than courteous to any bigshot from the Agency, regardless of the fact that they brought him most of DFI's business. Under normal circumstances he would treat them pretty much like shit but take their business, anyway.

Right now he was too preoccupied to put on the bad-guy act.

"Mr. Simpson," the man said when he was close. "So good to see you."

Luke was tempted to ignore his outstretched hand but let the notion pass. It wasn't this guy's fault he had dropped in at a bad time. He was doubtless under orders like everyone else. He shook his hand. "Howdy."

"Howdy to you. Devlin, Agency Intelligence. Can we talk somewhere?"

"Sure. Talk."

He blinked. He was a young guy in his twenties, painfully skinny under a baggy blue suit, deathly pale, the kind of guy Luke guessed would wear a turtleneck sweater and groove on classical piano when not pushing paper for the government. Certainly not your typical agent, this Ivy League boy. "This may take awhile," Devlin said uneasily. His eyes went to the deck, where the fringe on the patio umbrella waved lightly in the breeze from the copter. "We might want to get out of the sun."

"I have company," Luke said. "And not much time for you."

"Oh." He nodded, looking around. He seemed bewildered. "So this is Deadly Force, huh? The Director told me you had quite an impressive little military base here. I'm afraid I don't see anything."

"You see what you need to see." Luke sighed. "Look, I really do have a lot of things going on right now. Could you come to the point?"

"Surely. I have been given to understand that you specialize in domestic activities, preferring not to work out-of-country. I have further been given to understand that you work clandestinely, rather dearly, but with great alacrity."

Luke's hackles began to rise involuntarily. It was this kind of beating around the bush, this kind of politician's bullshit instead of straight talk, that had helped drive him from the Agency. This guy, Devlin, was trying to say that Luke was good, kept his mouth shut, but cost a lot. Luke bit his tongue to cut off what was about to come out and nodded instead.

"The Director asked me to approach you with a problem. It's not a great problem, and certainly nothing we couldn't handle ourselves with ease, but nevertheless a problem. A minor problem, probably, but still a problem."

"Do tell." Luke eyed him fiercely. "The point, Devlin."

"We're approaching you as a last resort before calling for congressional inquiry. We've notified the FBI, which claims that it's a police matter. But the Chicago police don't seem to be concerned. We feel it necessary to exhaust all means at our disposal before taking this to Capitol

Hill. We perceive a problem, and therefore one *must* exist.''

"I see.'' Luke reached out suddenly, took Devlin's limp right hand in his own, and began to shake it vigorously. "Thank you so much for coming. Thank you so, so much.'' He dropped his hand, grinning at him, beaming. "Good-bye now. Good-bye, and take care.''

He turned on his heel, grumbling under his breath, and stalked toward the cabin.

"Mr. Simpson?''

Luke waved him off. He heard Devlin's timid footsteps running after him. Devlin appeared at his elbow, jogging sideways. "Perhaps I haven't made myself clear. We're offering you employment.''

"I'm rich already,'' Luke growled. "Why would I want a job?''

"I was made to believe you do this kind of thing by trade.''

Luke stopped. He turned. "Do what kind of thing, Devlin? You haven't told me why you're here yet. You haven't said a word that's made sense. You're talking in circles, and that pisses me off. Go away and leave me alone.''

He turned and walked again. He saw Missy's face in the kitchen window. She looked so old for her age, so sad.

"Wait,'' Devlin cried. "I have important business!''

"Shove it,'' Luke snapped back at him.

"We suspect a foreign power is creating civil unrest in a major American urban center!'' Devlin caught up to him again, red-faced and spluttering. "What I mean, dammit, is that the Russians are trying to cause a race riot. That is what I mean.''

Luke stopped. He looked at Devlin, incredulous. "You guys have really lost it,'' he said, and laughed. "What could the Russians gain by that?''

"They could gain by spreading urban unrest. Make it another long hot summer, like 1968. Blacks against whites, total chaos in every major city. Our society ripping apart at the seams just as another Berlin crisis develops in Europe, one we're too preoccupied to deal with decisively. Who knows? The point is, something is happening in Chicago. We sent an operative there and lost him."

Luke started. "Chicago?"

"Yes. That seems to be the flashpoint."

"Why me? Why Deadly Force?"

"The Director has a hunch, that's all. Our man might have been the victim of random crime. It's the crime that's got us concerned, the unrest it's causing. It's tripled in the last two weeks. We need an experienced independent like yourself to assess the situation, to dig down deep and see what's at the root. We need someone like your Deadly Force."

Luke looked up at Missy again, waiting so patiently for her father to come back. Whatever had happened to him had started in Chicago. Whatever he had been running from was there. Larry Vandevere was a good cop, a smart cop. If he was scared enough to run all the way to Arizona, things had to be pretty bad. Bad enough, maybe, for Deadly Force to step in.

"You've got us," Luke said.

"Super." Devlin wiped his pale brow with his fingertips. He chuckled. "That wasn't so bad. I'd heard you were a real bear. Can we go inside now and hammer out the details? This sun is brutal."

Missy let out a sudden squeal. Luke glanced over, then followed her eyes to the sky. Jake was coming back, a dot above the reaching arms of the cactus on the western horizon, swooping out of the sky.

"I've got everything I need to know," Luke said to Devlin. "I'll be in touch."

"But . . ."

"Good-bye." Luke waited as Missy came down off the deck and ran to him, then took her hand and walked with her past the CIA helicopter to where Jake was landing. The Bensen bounced on the runway and rolled a dozen yards, trailed by a plume of dust. The motor wound down to a rattling chug, then stopped. Jake slumped forward against his restraining harness as if exhausted.

"He's alone," Missy said.

That's when Luke saw the blood.

Chapter 4

Dr. Tran Cao was a nervous wreck, a shattered man, a ruined shadow of his former self. And all because of a goddamn white paper tube and a bit of chopped-up weed inside.

He held up his slim hands and looked at them. They were shaking. He smelled his fingers. No trace of smoke there, no familiar yellow stains on the fingers of his right hand. It was like smelling the hands of a wax dummy. No character there, no personality. They had become a stranger's hands.

It was impossible to concentrate on the stereoscope on the table in front of him. He was examining low-resolution infrared satellite photos, frame by painstaking frame, and had been doing it since arriving at work that morning, seven long hours ago. He barely remembered why. Something about upper-strata coal deposits in Kentucky. He knew they showed up green on the film.

"God," he said to himself. He leaned against the back-rest of his steel International Resources Corporation chair. He felt giddy. His heart pounded. The need for a cigarette was like a low-grade fever, frying him slowly. He had quit a week ago, on July 10, dropped down from five packs a day on Thursday to zero on Friday. He barely remembered why. His starving lungs ached in his chest. His mouth tasted odd, bland, and fleshy. He was sweating.

Tran got up and paced his office. He stopped at the window to look out across Santa Monica Bay, found nothing of interest there in the familiar blue water and brown strand of shoreline ringed with palm trees, and resumed his pacing. He was thinking of Marlboros, how fresh they smelled in the pack, how firm they were between your lips, how marvelous the smoke was when inhaled. Only a masochist would quit this way. Tran had watched South Vietnam fall in ruin, had endured life as a refugee, had even been shot through the calf during the war. Pieces of cake, all of them, in comparison to this. This was an endless nightmare.

He sat back down and attempted to focus the stereo-scope. The intercom buzzed. He jerked in his chair, nearly fell out. He reached for the talk button, missed it, tried again, made it. "What?"

"A call on line four."

"Yeah? Who?"

"He didn't give his name."

"Goddamn, why not?"

Rose sighed. "I didn't ask."

"I'm busy," Tran shouted. "Lots to do. No time. Leave me alone."

"Line four," she snapped, and clicked off, mumbling something about nonsmokers.

Tran spun in his chair and found the phone. He snatched the receiver off its cradle. "Tran Cao. What you want?"

"Man," a deep voice replied, "your English is getting *bad*."

"Luke? Simpson?"

"Sure, Frags. Did I call at a bad time?"

Tran groaned. "It depends on what you want."

"I want you, man. Time to roll."

"Ah, hell, Luke. I don't think I can."

"Tied up with work?"

"No, I could get away. It's personal shit."

"Anything I can help with?"

Tran shrugged. "I doubt it. I turned forty, see."

"So? Happens to all of us, if we're lucky."

"Well, I quit smoking too. How do you say it? I quit cold turkey."

Luke laughed. "Not you, Frags. Anybody but you. How about the betel nut? Give that up too?"

Tran shivered. "Cold turkey. Seven days now. I hurt all over."

"Cal Steeples will dig that," Luke said, and laughed again. "Come on over to Arizona and we'll help you over the hump. I'll keep your mind occupied."

"Not on the Cray," Tran said. "I'm too—what do they say—I'm too spaced-out to work with *that* monster. Honest, Luke . . . my brain is cooking."

"Just a little Cray and that's all," Luke said. "A little wizardry, a little button pushing, a little of the fancy shit you do so well. I need you to interface with the FBI mainframe."

Tran ran a hand through his stiff black hair. "Have you got a feed?"

"That's what I need *you* for."

"You mean, I've got to make my own?"

"Can I expect you tonight, then?"

"Shit!"

"You'll have to rent a car at the airport in Phoenix. Jake's in no shape to pick you up. I've got company."

"Luke . . . Jesus!"

"Thanks, Frags. You're number one."

The phone went dead in his hand. Tran put it down and ran both hands through his hair. He made a sour face. He got up off his stool suddenly, went out into the hallway, and ran to the elevator. He punched the down button on the wall. When the doors slid open, he jumped inside, jammed a finger on the button marked *L*, and watched them slide shut. He waited impatiently until the doors slid open again, sprinted out into the hallway, and burst into the employee lounge.

A big brown National cigarette machine sat in the corner. Three people in white lab coats were at a table drinking coffee. They looked up at him uncertainly as he stalked over to it with his hand shoved deep inside his pants pocket.

His shaking fingers counted out six quarters. He dropped them through the slot. He pulled the lever, shoved it back, and a pack of Marlboros dropped into the tray. He picked it up and ripped the cellophane away. He tore the silver wrapping off the top. The aroma of fresh cigarettes drifted out. He tapped one out, thinking of his lungs, his heart, his hardening, forty-year-old arteries. He smiled with maniacal intent.

"Thanks a bundle, Luke," he muttered, and lit it up.

Calvin Steeples, founder, president, and sole employee of Steeples Aerial Services, was at that moment considering suicide.

Like Tran Cao, he had endured a lot in his life. Growing up poor and fatherless in a family of twelve had just been the start. Busting his ass to support himself while attending the four-year grind of UCLA had come in the middle. Later there had been the matter of the war, of his getting shot down, of his internment by the North Vietnamese for three years in a cage barely big enough to squat in. There had been the matter of seeing friends die. By the age of twenty-four, Calvin Steeples knew just how big and hard the world could be.

But now he was getting to know just how big and hard the government he had sacrificed so many years of his life for could be. The beginning of the end had appeared in his mailbox a few days ago. It was a letter from the IRS. Steeples Aerial Services was to be audited.

That simple.

"Jesus Christ!" Calvin howled. He made fists out of his large black hands and pounded his desk, which was tucked in one corner of the sparse little matchbox he called home, which was tucked in a nondescript corner of Los Angeles near the Municipal Airport. It was at the airport where he kept his crop duster, his only means of support, a Piper Cherokee that Uncle Sam would probably take from him when this audit was over. Hell, Uncle Sam would probably take the matchbox house, and the desk, and the man pounding his fists on it as well. Calvin Steeples was a lousy record keeper. Most of his business was done on a handshake. And if the truth be known, he had in fact paid almost no income tax because he simply didn't know how much money he made. He had a house, he had a car, he had beer in the refrigerator. There was usually money in his wallet.

He could see it all quite clearly in his mind. A phone call to arrange the audit. A bland-faced little fat man knocking on the door, toting a slim little briefcase and wearing thick horn-rimmed spectacles. A microscopic inspection of Calvin's ledgers, records, and receipts, of which there were about two. A headshake. A dirty look. A sigh.

A year to five in the slammer.

Calvin threw the drawers of his desk open for the fifth time. He searched them with his hands, moaning and sweating. It was late afternoon outside, and the hazy Los

Angeles sun cast dismal light through the window above the desk. It was hot in the house; the air conditioner had given up a few days ago, about the same time the letter from the IRS arrived. And wasn't it about then that the roof had started to leak?

"Oh, shit," Calvin said. He slammed the drawers shut and propped his face on his hands. Amazing, just amazing how what had seemed to be a good and prosperous life had suddenly turned out to be a hollow sham. He had built his empire on quicksand. And Charlene was supposed to come over tonight, was supposed to bring a duck and some champagne for a backyard barbecue. Why the hell she would want to barbeque a duck was beyond Calvin's comprehension, but Charlene was talented in other ways and entitled to her quirks. Yet how could he eat, how could he be good company, how could he best utilize her talents, with this hanging over his head? When would the call that would ruin his life come?

The phone rang.

He stared at it. He licked his lips. His left cheek twitched.

It rang again.

He reached for it slowly, his fingers spread wide. His arm shook. He had undergone torture as a POW, had flown through enemy ground fire, had crash-landed a C5-A into a rice paddy and calmly watched it burn. He'd been fifteen years younger then, fifteen pounds lighter then, a stranger to fear then. Now he was older, wiser, and knew that if there was one person in this world who could fuck you up worse than Victor Charlie, it was Uncle Sam.

The phone rang for the third time, shrill in the looming quiet.

He picked it up. "Yeah."

"This is the tax man," a gruff voice spoke. "Calvin, we wants yo' ass."

"Aw, Charlene," he said, and breathed again. "Don't be funny."

"Ha ha!" she sang out. She had a weird laugh, something like Ruth Buzzi's; Calvin had accepted it but it still grated on his ears. "Ha-haaaaa-haw-haw-haw!"

"What's up, babe?"

"You, I hope," she cooed. "We still on for tonight?"

He rolled his head, massaging the back of his neck with one hand. "I dunno, Char. I got a headache coming on."

"I can make it go away."

"Yeah. But after this tax thing is over, huh? I gotta go to the airport and dig through the Cherokee for paper."

"You putting me off?"

"Just this once, Char. Besides, I might have to spray tonight. The honeybees don't go in till dark, and I'm contracted for nine hundred acres of alfalfa."

"Dammit!" she screamed. That was something else about her Calvin couldn't grasp: the short fuse. If she wasn't laughing like a hyena, she was screeching like a loon. He was tired of the whole scene. "Damn you, Calvin Steeples! To think I bought my first duck for you! You'll never see me again! Never, ever!"

She slammed the phone down.

"Bet I will," he said, and hung up. He rubbed his face. Who really gave a shit?

The phone rang again. Calvin picked it up and stuck it tiredly to his ear. "Yes?"

"Hey, hotshot. You ready to roll?"

"Hi, Luke. What's up?"

"A strange one this time. I've got a buddy in trouble, and it looks like big trouble. I need you."

"Can it wait? I'm up to my ears in shit."

"We all are, Cal. Come on over and stand in my shit for a while. It'll clear your head."

Calvin shrugged. What the hell? If the fat man with the

briefcase couldn't find him, there couldn't be an audit. Not for a while, anyway. And the alfalfa wasn't going anywhere. Besides, working for Luke brought in verifiable bucks. And he would ask for a receipt this time.

"On the way," he said, and hung up.

Ben Sanchez was in deep shit himself.

The woman outside had a big nickel-plated revolver and one hell of a temper. She was covered with bruises. One eye was swollen shut. A cut on her cheek had crusted into lines of dried blood that looked like big stitches on her face. Under the fierce afternoon sun her eyes were wild and bright. She was staggering around the trailer like a drunk.

"Ben Sanchez, you son of a bitch!" she screamed. She raised the pistol and fired. Ben ducked. The window beside his head broke and crashed down on the living-room carpet in big shards. Ben's nine-year-old twins, hiding in the kitchen behind the counter, screeched and giggled. He heard his wife, Wanda, tell them to shush up.

He raised his head. "Drop the gun, Naomi. This isn't going to help Tom at all."

"*Bastard*!" She shot again. The bullet punched through the ceiling in the middle of the living room. Bits of ceiling tile and insulation dust rained down on the coffee table. Ben looked back, shaking his head grimly. Another hole for the Arizona rains to leak in. The trailer was in bad enough shape as it was.

He was still in his underwear. For two weeks he had been pulling night duty, patrolling the White Mountain Indian Reservation while the moon shined down on its taverns and dusty streets. The hardest things to contend with so far had been the late-night drunks and the boredom. Then, the previous night, this thing with Tom and Naomi Whitedeer had started. Tom was a big, barrel-chested man in his thirties. He worked off-reservation, at the Hightimber Sawmill in Huachuca. He liked his liquor straight out of the bottle. When he got to drinking after work, which was happening often lately, he either got cryingly morose, or he got mean. When he got mean, he took it out on Naomi. The night before was no exception. A neighbor called in to say Tom was at it again. Ben Sanchez was dispatched in the patrol Bronco, alone, to assess the situation.

He came in just as Tom was pounding Naomi over the head with a broken leg from a chair. Their three-room house, hot and reeking of spilled whiskey, was a shambles. There were fist-size holes in the walls. The TV lay on the floor, staring balefully at the wall, its metal sides dented. *Wheel of Fortune* played on it full blast. One of Naomi's roosters was perched on the antenna, calmly watching Tom hammer Naomi on the head. It stretched itself and flapped its wings as Ben burst through the door and wrestled the big man off his wife. It cackled and brayed as Ben snapped the handcuffs over Tom's thick wrists and hauled him outside.

That's when Naomi picked up a goldfish bowl that had miraculously survived the destruction and smashed it over Ben's head. "Leave my husband alone!" she had screamed. Ben went down in a flood of water and fish.

Nutty situation.

Ben rubbed the lump on the crown of his head now, peeking out the window at the crazy woman circling his trailer house. He had been trying to sleep in the daylight and the heat when she suddenly started shooting up the trailer. Tom was down at the station, sleeping it off on a cot. He would miss a day's work, have a ferocious hangover, be warned not to do it anymore. A month or two down the road, it would happen all over again. It was pretty predictable. But no one could have predicted Naomi would take it so hard this time.

She shot again. The vase full of red silk roses on the coffee table burst apart.

"Stop it, Naomi," Ben called out.

"*I want my husband back!*"

"You'll get him tonight."

"*Now!*"

She shot out another windowpane. Apparently she had brought a pocketful of bullets, because Ben had counted eight shots already. This might go on for hours. His police revolver was in the bedroom in its holster, where it would stay. He could hardly shoot Naomi. He had known her, like all of the other Native Americans on the reservation, all his life.

"Put the gun down, Naomi."

Blam! The kitchen light fixture exploded like a glass bomb. The twins, Bobby and Darla, shrieked and laughed. This was the most fun they had had all summer.

Wanda tried to be helpful. "Why don't you come in and have some coffee," she shouted out. "I'll make a fresh pot."

Pow! The mirror on the living room wall this time. Ben crawled over to the telephone and plucked it down off its table. Enough of this. Time to call for a backup.

The phone was dead when he put it to his ear. He jiggled the buttons. He knocked it against the floor and put it to his ear again.

"Hello?" someone said. "Hello?"

"Who's this?" Ben asked.

"Luke. Man, have you got mystic powers. It didn't even ring."

"My grandfather was a medicine man. What's up?"

"How's your Spanish?"

"Kinda rusty."

"Brush up on it and drive on up here. We're under contract again."

Kablooey! Chunks of ceiling tile pattered down on Ben's head. "I'm kinda tied up, Luke."

"Sounds like a war. Can you get off work for a few days?"

"Hell, I can't even get out of my trailer!"

"See you in a couple hours, then. Bye."

Ben hung up. Naomi was around back now, screaming and cursing. More glass broke. Wanda would have to see about getting some plywood to cover the holes while he was gone. With luck, though, it wouldn't even rain until he got back. Then he would have enough money to buy some new glass, fix the holes in the roof, and make a couple trailer payments. It was probably a good thing Luke was around, even though he did tend to call at inopportune times.

Kapow! A flower pot hanging from a macramé rope burst apart and clattered down on the kitchen linoleum. The twins howled.

Ben picked the receiver back up and dialed his station.

By evening, Jake O'Bannion was finally drunk enough. He preferred it to the noxious-smelling knockout gas Luke offered him, the same gas they had used on terrorists in Mexico the previous year. He preferred it, also, to undergoing any kind of surgery in Phoenix. People die in hospitals, he said. Just do it and get it over with.

He was belting out "My Wild Irish Rose" at the top of his lungs when Luke and Missy went to work on him. Missy mopped his leg with a towel while Luke used a pair of disinfected tweezers to dig the buckshot out. Some of the shot was nestled in his shinbone. Most of it was buried an inch deep in the hard muscle of his calf. His iliac artery was intact, but still he bled like a pig. Luke knew he would be one stiff son of a bitch for a few weeks.

When they were done, Luke injected him with penicillin obtained from the copious medical supplies stored in the compound underground. As a final measure before wrapping him up, Luke poured a whole bottle of iodine over the wound.

Jake never missed a beat.

Larry Vandevere squinted into the sudden wedge of sunlight that flooded across his face. He had been in the trunk for five hours now, and had begun to think of it as the place he would die. It was hot, for one thing. He was bathed in sweat, his shirt and pants pasted to his body like a squishy second skin. It stank, for another thing. His head pounded from smelling exhaust fumes. His back ached from lying across the jack. His knuckles were bloody from pounding on the trunk lid. But overshadowing all of this was the overwhelming need to know what had been going on since the two men threw him in the trunk and slammed the lid down.

He saw shapes standing in the light. He sat up, already looking past them for a sign of Missy. He saw an expanse of concrete, and small planes parked in a row. A Cessna buzzed overhead. A small airport, then. The desert stretched around it, undulating in the heat.

They were looking down at him. Hands reached in and jerked him out. He stood on the concrete, wobbling, squinting, looking around for Missy.

"Where's she at?" he said. His head throbbed.

"None of your business," one of them said. He was not a stranger to Larry. It was Rudy Vasquez, Chicago PD detective, known to Missy as Rudy the Rat. And he *was* a rat: a cop gone bad.

Larry saw the blood on his face. He swung around and looked at the other man. Old blood on his shoulder. Larry had heard distant gunshots several hours ago. Who had done that?

"Come on," Rudy said.

They forced him away from the car. He broke away and ran around to the side, looking frantically inside for Missy. A shotgun lay on the floor. He had heard that, too, booming like a cannon. There was blood on the front seat. Theirs or hers? He straightened.

"Did she get away?"

Rudy and the other man stared at him dully. They seemed exhausted, weary from their wounds. In the distance behind them, a white Learjet swooped down onto the runway, soundlessly touching down.

"Did she?"

"Goddammit, your daughter's all right, Larry," Rudy said. "You know I wouldn't hurt her."

"Sure." Larry sneered at him bitterly. "But then, I thought I knew you pretty well."

Rudy looked at the ground between his feet. The Learjet rolled down the runway behind him, coming closer. The noise of its engine was a distant, whistling howl. The other man looked back at it, then turned and motioned to Larry. "That's the one. Let's go."

They took Larry's arms and pulled him forward. He wrenched himself free again. He leaned inside the car and fetched the shotgun out. It was easy, he knew, far too easy. He turned and leveled it at them.

"Back off, guys."

The man smirked. Rudy shook his head ruefully.

Larry lowered the shotgun. The Learjet lumbered close and stopped. "Not loaded?" he shouted over the noise.

"Be real," the man said. He dug in his slacks pocket and produced a single red shell, which he held up. He was a young guy, maybe twenty-five, with dark greasy hair and squinty little eyes. A real wise-ass, Larry decided. How Rudy had fallen in with his type, Larry couldn't imagine. He was suddenly very tired of him, tired of being chased halfway across the country by him, tired of running in fear from him.

He dropped the shotgun and lunged toward him. Before the young man could react, Larry drove a fist hard into his jaw, knocking him backward. He spun on his heels and fell down.

"Ah, Larry," Rudy said. "Don't."

The hatch on the Learjet fell open. Someone leaned out and pointed a pistol. "Enough of that," he shouted.

Rudy put a hand on Larry's arm. "Don't fight it," he said. "You know it won't do any good."

Larry punched him in the face.

Chapter 5

"It's nice to have you all together again," Luke said. He lifted his glass. Tonight he was drinking Jack Daniel's, iceless in a juice glass, as warm as the balmy night breeze that blew in from the moonlit desert.

"Here's to us," he said.

They lifted their glasses: Tran Cao, Calvin Steeples, Ben Sanchez, and Jake O'Bannion, just sobering up from his operation but willing to drink one more with old friends. The moonlight slanting down from the sky cast stark black shadows across the redwood deck of the A-frame. Out on the desert, the saguaro stood watch, tall and silent in the gusting night breeze. It was ten o'clock.

They drank. Ice clinked in glasses. Missy stood by, close to where Luke sat, uncertain of all these strangers. She was dead on her feet but hadn't been able to sleep, though Luke had given her his bed and she had tried. He couldn't blame her. Somewhere out there in the darkness, her father was in the hands of strangers.

"When each of you got here, I told you roughly what we're up against," Luke said, setting his glass on the

table. "We've got a good friend of mine in the trunk of
somebody's car. That alone is reason enough to get DFI
together and start scouring the country, but there's more
involved."

Calvin Steeples sat up straighter in his patio chair.
"Yeah. The Russians in Chicago." He laughed. "My
ass."

"My ass too," Luke said, giving him a grin. "The CIA
boy they flew out here said the director had a hunch, only
a hunch. He can't sell Congress what he can't prove. They
can hardly justify diverting money and operatives to a
domestic investigation on a hunch."

"Especially one as screwy as this," Calvin said. He
leaned to the side and spat across the deck to the sand
below. "That's why they called us in. They lost a man,
they don't know how, they don't know why. He might
have slipped on a banana peel and fell down a manhole,
for all they know. So, like true politicians, instead of
going in full steam and taking care of the problem, they
back off and let somebody else do it."

Jake O'Bannion sat up and snorted. "Sounds like the
war you guys all fought in." He hiccupped and sagged
back into his chair. Missy giggled at him. Luke saw him
give her a wink.

"Right," Luke said. "And the way the Agency boy
talked, they've got a war going on in Chicago right now.
A crime war."

"What's the tie-in?" Tran Cao asked. He puffed on his
cigarette thoughtfully. "Your friend came halfway across
the country to find you. The same day, the CIA arrives.
Your friend is from Chicago, and the CIA is worried about
Russians in Chicago. Your friend is kidnapped, and Jake
gets his leg blown to pieces. Busy day, I'd say." He
leaned toward Jake. "Does it hurt much, old friend?"

Jake grunted. "Only when I'm dancing."

Even Ben Sanchez, normally quiet, chuckled at this. A nondrinker, he was nursing an iced tea. He stared at his glass with a reflective smile. "There's a tie-in," he said. "Luke's friend is a cop. Cops don't run unless they're in a situation they can't handle alone, and then they run for a backup. That's what that Vandevere guy was doing. He needed a backup."

"Why us?" Calvin asked. "Why not his own people?"

"That's what we need to find out," Luke said. "Tran, I need all the statistics on the crime situation in Chicago. The FBI stats will be old, but we're going back a few weeks, anyhow. We need to see just where this is happening, and how big it is. After that, tap in to the Chicago central computer directly, and see how they correlate. Do you want to fire up the Cray now, or start in the morning?"

Tran groaned. "Considering how long it will take just to patch in, I'd better start tonight. Got any clues to the access code?"

Luke grinned. "The Cray will give you a hundred thousand possibilities a minute."

"But the possible combinations are infinite, Luke. It could take me an infinite number of years."

"Teenage hackers do it to banks every day, Tran, and that's after school. I'd say start with a random numeric string, chop it into ten-digit blocks, feed it to see what bites, and go down the line."

"Why ten digits?"

"That's just to start. Then go to eleven, then twelve, and so on."

Tran shook his head. "I hope you don't mind a million-dollar phone bill."

"No sweat. I'll bill it to the Agency."

Ben chuckled again, and Luke turned to him. "You seem to be in an unusual mood tonight."

The Apache spread his arms. "Why not? My trailer's

shot to shit, my wife's pissed because I left again, my chief's threatening to fire me for missing work, and you make lousy iced tea. What else could go wrong?''

Luke shrugged. ''Your plane could crash.''

''What plane?''

''The United out of Sky Harbor International tonight at one-fifteen. Your ticket to O'Hare is at the counter, *señor*.''

''*Señor*?''

''Missy's dad worked the South Side until a few days ago, Ben. There's a large Hispanic section there. We need to know from the inside what's going on. Try to get a line on the criminal element, see if they're involved, and if they are, what's motivating them. Cal, same for you on the black side.''

Calvin smirked good-naturedly. ''Stereotyped again.''

''Sorry, guys. We need to work every angle we can. I'll be following up on the license number Jake got as soon as the Department of Motor Vehicles opens. It's an Illinois plate, probably a rental. So maybe we've got a tie-in here, and maybe we don't. Either way, we've got a lot of legwork to do before we can start building assumptions.''

''Ouch,'' Jake said. ''Don't say *leg*.''

Luke smiled. ''Your head will be hurting so bad in the morning, you won't notice your leg at all. And I've got you booked to Chicago tonight too.''

''You're kidding.''

''You and Ben and Cal can pick up some crutches at an all-night drugstore in Phoenix on the way to Sky Harbor. I need you to find out what things look like from the cops' side of the fence. Know anybody on the force there?''

''The Windy City PD? Hardly.''

''Well, make some fast friends.'' Luke drained his glass and refilled it from the bottle on the table. ''And one last thing, gentlemen, before we go our separate ways.'' He turned to Missy. "Will you get me those papers off the desk I showed you? And a couple of pens too."

Missy went inside, came back a moment later to hand Calvin, Ben, and Tran Cao papers and pens.

"Standard free-lance contracts, as always," Luke said. "Sign wherever you find a dotted line."

Ben scowled. "Why is it," he said, "that you always seem to hand these out in the dark?"

Luke grinned wickedly. "My lawyer recommended it."

At 3:10 that night, two south Chicagoans were murdered in a particularly ghastly way.

The perpetrators, who would never be caught, were Rodney and Jamaica Jones. Rodney and Jamaica were teenage brothers who did not happen to share the same father. Between them they had committed over eighty crimes, ranging from purse snatching to rape to aggravated assault to murder. Both had spent considerable time in juvenile detention. Neither had ever held a job. Neither intended to. The crime business was just too lucrative.

Especially lately.

They entered the crumbling redbrick tenement at 150th Street and Dillmore by means of the back door, which had been broken off its hinges years before and never repaired. In their pockets they each had one thousand dollars in crisp new bills. They moved purposefully to the second floor, their young faces fixed and intent, two shadows skulking down a scarred and ruined hallway. They came to the first door and kicked it open. Others in the building would later speculate about why they had chosen the second floor instead of the first, why they had chosen the first door on the left instead of the one on the right. The police would not speculate at all because the police never came.

A woman squawked, somewhere in a back bedroom. Rodney and Jamaica froze in the dark, tense, their faces

shiny with sweat. A moment later she came out, a mon-
strously fat woman wearing a bra and panties. A baby
began to cry.

The woman saw the two young men and squawked
again. She turned and hustled away. They heard her opening drawers. Silverware rattled. She came back with a
large knife.

"Just back on out that door," she cried in a trembling
voice.

Rodney and Jamaica laughed. They lunged for her, and
when she swung the knife in a clumsy arc, Rodney knocked
it out of her hand. Jamaica hit her on the side of the head
with his fist and she fell down.

"Fuckin' bitch," he murmured. He kicked her. "The
man says move out, bitch. The man been tellin' you that
for too long. Can't you hear the man when he talk?"

He bent down, picked up the knife, jerked her head up
by the hair, and cut one of her ears off. It stuck on the
knife and he flipped it away. "You hear me now, bitch?"

She opened her mouth and howled. Blood drizzled down
her neck, black and shiny in the murky dark. Rodney
moved back and flipped the light on. He shut the door with
his foot.

"Now we gonna fuck you up *good*," he whispered.

They turned her over on her back. It was like manhan-
dling a beached whale, and Jamaica giggled involuntarily as
he strained against her. She trembled and moaned, looking
up at them with huge brown eyes. The baby in the bedroom screeched.

Jamaica, perhaps a bit more gutsy than his younger
brother, perhaps a little higher on the PCP they had snorted,
bent and placed the tip of the knife blade on the woman's
cheek below her eye. He held it there, seeming to mull
things over, breathing hard.

Then he jammed the knife under her huge frightened eye and pried it out of her head.

She jerked and flopped. Rodney put his foot over her mouth and let her scream into the sole of his sneaker. Jamaica levered the knife up and down, amazed that the human eyeball was anchored to the socket with so many stringy muscles. He gave up and stabbed her through the other eye. Clear fluid squirted out.

The man who gave them the thousand dollars each had said to scare the shit out of people, make them think. The Jones boys figured this was the best way.

The baby howled in the other room. Jamaica went in with the knife. Rodney stared down at the woman, no longer needing to stand on her mouth, revolted and amazed. Her teeth were chattering. He wiped his foot on the rug.

The baby's crying abruptly stopped. Jamaica came out. His shirt had bleeding lines on it, as if someone had shot him with a squirt gun full of blood. He was grinning, but it was a sick grin. "Fucked 'em up," he said, looking back in the bedroom, then down at the woman. He seemed dazed. "Fucked 'em up, all right."

He walked over and stabbed the woman in the stomach. She gasped. She jerked. He stabbed her again, frowning. She attempted a laborious sit-up. Blood trickled out of her mouth. Jamaica stabbed her again.

Rodney had had enough of this. His guts were getting queasy. "Let's go," he said.

Jamaica straightened. He wiped his face with his arm. "Okay," he said, and dropped the knife.

They left, moving fast, looking over their shoulders in the hot, narrow hallway, as if afraid of ghosts.

Luke woke up at first light. He sat up on the couch, blinking the sleep out of his eyes. The golden hands of the deadwood clock said five-fifteen. He got up and peeked into the bedroom where Missy was sleeping, satisfied himself that she was all right, and went into the kitchen to make coffee for himself and Tran. The Vietnamese doctor had been down below with the Cray since midnight and could probably use a cup. Watching the huge Cray, a surplus job Luke had picked up for a small fortune in New Mexico, perform its two hundred million operations per second was about as interesting as watching a test pattern on TV.

With a steaming cup in each hand, he went out into the cool of the desert dawn and walked across the macadam-ized airstrip to the stone outcropping at the far side that marked the central entrance to Superstition's Base. Strain-ing not to spill the coffee, using his little finger, he punched in the access code on a small panel recessed in the rock and waited as three inch-thick chromium steel bolts withdrew themselves from the jamb back into the door. Effortlessly he pushed the massive steel door open with his elbow and walked into the dim, sloping tunnel bored out of solid rock that led to the underground cham-bers and Tran Cao.

He caught him asleep at the console of the Cray. The huge computer blinked and whirred, feeding random num-bers into a phone tie-in to the FBI at a staggering rate. An overflowing ashtray was parked beside his elbow. The whole cavern already stank of stale smoke.

"Continental breakfast," Luke said, nudging his chair. "Hope you drink it black."

"Huh?" Tran jerked upright, then grinned sheepishly. "Just inspecting my eyelids for holes." He accepted the cup. "Man, but this is boring shit."

"I know. But you've got to be ready to jump if we happen on the right code."

Tran yawned. "Why not just ask your Agency buddies for it? This could take years."

"Well, first of all, I doubt that they have it. You've got to remember that there are two competing agencies here, neither one too full of admiration for the other. Second of all, why would any government man worth his salt hand the code over to a group of maladjusted mercenary types like us? We're lunatic fringe reactionaries in their book."

"But they seem to need our services a lot."

"I think they're beginning to rely on us. We haven't let them down yet."

Tran fumbled in his shirt pocket for his cigarettes, nodding. He lit one up. "How's the little girl?"

"Sleeping. I'll go topside in a minute and keep her company. Unless you want to, and I'll spell you here."

"No, not me. I don't know what to say around kids."

"Neither do I, really. Especially in a situation like this, with her dad missing."

Tran blew smoke thoughtfully. "Doesn't she have any relatives you could dump her off on? Where's her mother?"

Luke winced internally. "Dead."

"Hmm. How about Grandma and Grandpa?"

"I don't know. I think I'll just keep her until this is over. She won't get in the way."

"In a case like this, probably not. We're playing detective more than anything else. How come the Agency handed us this one, anyway? It doesn't seem to be up our usual alley."

"Because those two competing agencies are careful as hell not to step on each other's toes. The CIA has its suspicions, but Chicago crime is really the FBI's responsibility. The FBI thinks it's a police matter, so everybody is just handing it off to each other. Like I said, the Agency relies on us now. We've proven that we can do what they can, only better and cleaner. And if we get caught, the Director can pass us off as lunatics working for nobody but ourselves. Either way, they walk away squeaky clean."

"And we walk away with the money. Either way."

"They do pay good rates."

Tran worked on his cigarette some more, puffing it fiercely, looking cross-eyed at the burning tip. Smoke drifted up in thick clouds, slowly pulled along by the ventilation system. Overhead, the huge cargo net that caught falling rock chunks hung like a giant spider's creation, stretched from wall to wall. No fresh boulders in it, Luke noted gratefully. They were a bitch to get down.

"So," Tran said, "if we do crack the FBI's safe, what kind of valuables do we take out? Just dry statistics?"

Luke nodded. "That, and more. And in the meantime I need you to get the Cray working on something else. Remember that license plate number Jake got? I need it traced."

"FBI again?"

"Hardly. Try the Illinois Department of Motor Vehicles."

"Access code?"

"Try sweet-talking them on the phone first. Tell them you're with the Santa Monica PD. When that fails, and it will, start the Cray on another line with four-digit strings."

Tran sighed. "Numeric?"

"Numeric—alphanumeric—who knows?"

"Why four digits, then?"

"Call it a hunch."

Tran wearily crushed his cigarette into the ashtray. "I have a hunch I'll be here ten years from now."

Luke patted him on the shoulder and made his way back outside. The sun was just topping the mountains as he stepped out of the tunnel; it looked like it would be another glorious day. He finished his coffee and let the cup dangle from his finger as he walked back to the cabin. He assumed Missy would sleep till noon after the long, frantic days that had just passed for her. That would give him plenty of time to take a shower, shave, and get her something nice made for breakfast.

Jake, Ben, and Cal would be calling in soon with a progress report; with any luck Tran would gain access to at least one government computer, and they would have something to go on.

And with more luck, Larry would stay alive long enough for them to find him.

He made a disgusted face as he went up the steps to the deck. They were relying too much on luck here. But what other choice was there? Like Tran said, this kind of operation wasn't really up DFI's usual alley. With the ninety-foot satellite dish nestled in the mountains just east of here, they could communicate with the best tracking satellite currently in orbit, could intercept communications from around the world, could focus in on an ant in Zambia if they had to. But what good did that do when the target was locked in the trunk of somebody's car?

He went inside and found Missy sitting at the counter with her chin on her hands. Her face was puffy from sleep, her eyes bright with tears. She was staring out the window and glanced at Luke as he came in.

"Morning, Missy," Luke said. He put his cup down and fidgeted uncertainly. "Sleep okay?"

She shrugged. In Jake's drawstring pajamas she looked frail and small.

"I'll make breakfast," he said.

She turned to him. "Will you find him?"

"We'll sure try, honey."

A tear spilled down her cheek. "When?"

Luke tried to smile. "As soon as we can. Just as soon as we can."

"Oh, I *miss* him," she cried, and suddenly slid off her stool to run to Luke. She threw her arms around his waist and pressed her face to his stomach, sobbing.

"There, there," Luke said. His hands hovered over her helplessly. Timidly he stroked her hair. "We'll find him, Missy. Even if we have to tear up the whole damn country. We'll find him."

Of all the cabs waiting at the arrival gate at O'Hare, Jake O'Bannion had to pick this one.

It was a rusting old Checker, badly in need of a tuneup, desperately in need of a muffler. Tooling down the JFK Expressway, it left behind a dense trail of oily smoke in the morning air. It bounced on bad shocks like a cheap carnival ride. The backseat, where Jake sat in the first stages of motion sickness, was a horror of ruined uphol- stery, mashed cigarette butts, and discarded bubble gum. And to top things off, the driver had B.O.

"Shit-ass way to run things," he was saying. "You got Mayor Washington fighting the City Council, the City Council fighting each other, and the poor man on the bottom, you and me, getting the shit-ass end of things." He waved his arms as he drove. "Gimme Jane Byrne any day. A stony old bitch, probably the world's worst lay, but one tough broad. She knows how shit-ass things are. Hell, she was part of the goddamn *system*, and still knows it's a crock of shit. You understand what I'm saying, Pops?"

"Guess so," Jake mumbled, looking woozily out the smudgy window. Dawn hung over Chicago, pink and purple. Already at this hour, the expressway was full. Downtown Chicago rose on the horizon, shrouded in smog. Jake rubbed his face, stifling a groan. Luke had been right. His head pounded worse than his leg.

"But you talk about shit-ass—you shoulda seen the goddamn election. Not this one, but the one before. You say you're from New York, huh? Who you got there, that Koch guy? Creep. Probably a damn sight better than the fat son of a bitch we got. Bastard. What's with the crutches, anyway? Busted leg?''

Jake sighed. ''Yeah.''

''Reminds me of the time I sprained my ankle in Palmer Park. Stepped on a shit-ass apple core some jerk dropped on the cement. God, I thought I'd die. I think I passed out. You ever passed out, Pops? Just from pain, I mean? Like that?''

Jake stared at the back of his head, wishing the man would sprain a vocal cord. He was a fat guy in a dirty white T-shirt. He had a flattop haircut full of dandruff. And he smelled like, like—well, like a fat slob. Jake shrugged to himself. Guys like this came by the dozen. But did they all have to drive cabs?

''So, like, I woke up flat on my back staring up at the swing-sets. And my ankle . . . *Jeeeezzzz!* Talk about fucking *pain!*''

Yeah, talk about it, Jake thought. His leg throbbed like an impacted tooth; his head swelled and shrank, swelled and shrank. The hazy morning sun shafted light through his eyeballs like hot lightning. He stifled another groan. So much for Wild Turkey as a painkiller.

The cabbie talked and drove. The JFK Expressway dived underground to become a tunnel. When they came into the morning light again, Chicago's heart lay to the left, a hub pierced roughly through the center by the gigantic Sears Tower. Jake looked at the scene without enthusiasm. Big city or not, it still couldn't hold a candle to NYC. He felt a surprising twinge of homesickness then. Maybe one of these days he ought to get back there and touch base with his old precinct. But then again, maybe not. He had tried that routine once before and found that too much had changed. The young generation of cops that had taken the place of the old just didn't seem to give a shit about old-timers full of old-timer's tales. They were too busy making their own memories.

"Metro police, huh?" the cabbie said after a brief silence.

"Yeah."

"Hell of a fare, all the way from O'Hare. Hey, that rhymes." He laughed. "Now I'm a fucking poet. Twinkle twinkle, little star . . ."

Shut the fuck up, Jake thought savagely. His head felt ready to split. He gathered his crutches together. "Just let me out here."

"Here? Okey-doke." He veered hard to the curb and stopped. Cars honked. He showed them the finger. "Let's see. O'Hare to here, say thirty miles. Meter's busted, you know. Fifty bucks."

"Fifty bucks? You're kidding."

"Black and White woulda charged you eighty. Me, I'm cut-rate. Fifty bucks."

"I didn't just get off the boat, mister. Here's twenty." He dug out his wallet and produced a crisp new Andrew Jackson out of the sheaf of bills Luke had given him for the trip.

The cabbie sighed, ignoring it. "It don't work that way in Chicago, Pops. You pay what the cabbie tells you to, or you wear your teeth on the back of your head. If you get my drift."

Jake dropped the twenty to the seat and opened his door. The movement caused his leg to howl angrily. He ducked to get out, and his head responded with a brutal thump that made his eyes water.

He felt the driver lay a warm hand on his arm. "I seen the wad you got, Pops. It's eighty bucks now, or I lay you out like a Persian rug."

"Pop this, asshole." With a swift motion Jake grabbed his thumb and pressed it backward until it touched his forearm. There was a small, wet snap as his metacarpal bone broke.

"*Aaaiiieeee!*" the man blurted. He stared at his thumb, which was now pointing impossibly backward. The color washed out of his fat face. "You fucking bum! You broke my thumb!"

"You're right," Jake said. "You *are* a poet."

He climbed out, feeling his years and his wounds but grinning in spite of them. Down the street, he could see a line of police cars parked in front of an ornate sandstone building. He was positioning his crutches under his arms when the driver's door was hurled open. The driver jumped out and began to scream.

"Police! Help! Police!"

The few passersby on the sidewalk at this hour turned to gawk, then scuttered away as if witnessing a murder. The cabbie screamed for help at the top of his lungs. Down the street, red lights began to flash.

"Oh, shit" Jake breathed.

They got there quick. They listened to the cabbie's story, then to Jake's. He told them he was a retired cop, told them he was being fleeced by this no-good fat-assed jerk, and would they please go on about their beeswax and leave him alone?

The cabbie drove off to find a hospital.

They hauled Jake off for assault and battery.

Chapter 6

Ben Sanchez wasn't liking this one bit.

He had parked his rental car in a parking garage near West Pullman Park and begun to walk south. Three- and five-story tenement buildings squatted row upon row on either side of the street, built so close together that only a few ragged weeds had room to grow in the dead, trash-littered space between. Rusting fire escapes adorned sooty brick walls emblazoned with multicolored graffiti; TV antennas sprouted from roofs in skeletal disarray. Windows were mostly cardboard here. Broken glass sparkled dirtily on the cracked sidewalks. Some buildings were charred and gutted shells, like the ruins of war. In the oppressive morning heat the decayed smell of the city hung like thin gas. He had found the Spanish sector of the South Side.

As an Apache of the Chiricahua tribe, Ben felt some small sense of affinity with the Hispanics who had come to the United States. Most of the Mexicans working their way north were of mostly Indian blood, but it was a blood that had become watered with time. They no longer knew what tribe their ancestors sprang from, whether Incan or Mayan or Aztec. They no longer spoke the ancient tongues, having abandoned them centuries ago for the language of the conquistadores. They no longer cared for Indian ways, no longer taught their children their Indian heritage. So although Ben felt brothered with them in a small way, he felt no special love for the people of Mexico who had left the misery of their homeland to travel north in search of hope.

He felt no special love for the three punks following him, either.

They had begun dogging him four blocks ago, at the intersection of Wentworth and LaSalle Streets, skulking out of a shadowy alley into the hazy morning light as he passed. He took them in with one sideways glance: a tall one with greased-back hair and a shiny stud earring; a medium-sized one wearing a black headband pulled low over his eyes; and a short, fat one in an Army fatigue jacket. All in their late teens.

Ben nodded to himself. The three bears, out for a little morning stroll, a little morning action. They knew a stranger when they saw one.

He kept a steady pace, aware of their footfalls behind him. They were speaking to each other in a loud, slangy mix of English and Spanish. Ben came upon a knot of small children playing on the sidewalk. They looked up as he came toward them, then looked back at the three bears. Their laughter and chatter ceased. They scrambled aside, leaving a battered tricycle and a skateboard in the way. Ben stepped around them.

Five steps later he heard the tricycle crash over. One of the bears had kicked it aside. The skateboard flipped through the air and bounced in the street. One steel wheel snapped off and rolled madly away, scattering ball bearings.

Ben looked back. The tall one with the earring flashed him a leering smile. He reached in his jeans pocket as he walked and brought out a switchblade. Still smiling, he held it up and clicked the blade out for Ben to see. It glittered in the early sunlight. He made come-here motions with his head.

Ben sighed. He had crossed onto their turf—that much was obvious. For these three the entire world consisted of perhaps one square mile of southern Chicago, and for this square mile they would fight and kill and die. Like the Indians, the Hispanics harbored a fierce sense of territoriality. Someone had trespassed, someone with curiously high cheekbones, a bristly haircut, and reddish Indian features.

It occurred to Ben that maybe this was just what he was looking for.

He turned but stood his ground. Five paces separated them. Ben could see the silk of teenage whiskers on the cheeks of the tall one.

The three exchanged sly glances. The short one wiggled his finger for Ben to come closer.

"Fuck you," Ben said. It was the universal language of contempt, the best medium in the world. He turned on his heel and walked away.

"Hey, man," one of them shouted in Spanish. "Who do you think you are?"

Ben walked. The heels of his snakeskin boots clicked on the ruined sidewalk.

"I'm talking to you, son of a bitch!"

Ben raised another universal sign over his shoulder.

"*Ora de vamos a patalier el fundio!*"

Ben turned his head and grinned. "Yo mama, asshole."

They ran for him. Ben waited until they were close, then spun around. The face of the fat one was the first in his line of vision; Ben jabbed reflexively out with his open right hand and stiff-armed him in the throat. He emitted a sound like a loud burp and flipped over backward, his heels blurring in the air. A second later he thumped down on the sidewalk and lay there twitching.

The medium-sized guy, mama bear, hooked an arm around Ben's neck and spun in a clumsy circle. Ben was jerked backward. He found his balance, reached over his head, caught him by the ears.

The guy yelped. Ben hoisted him by the ears and flipped him overhead. He landed on his feet, clapped his hands to the sides of his head, tilted his face to the sky, and screamed.

The tall one backed off, crouching low. He worked the knife in slow figure eights, circling Ben. He thrust forward, feinting. Ben didn't flinch. In the young man's hard and shiny eyes he could see simple animal cunning and boundless hate, the two prerequisites for survival here. Yet the kid couldn't be more than seventeen. For Ben it was like looking at a time-machine image of himself. The prerequisites for survival in the White Mountain Reservation had been no different.

The kid lunged forward again, swooping the knife horizontally. Ben sucked in his stomach. The blade zipped harmlessly over his shirt, clicking as it struck a button. The tall kid backed away, grinning. He held the knife up to catch the sunlight, rolling it in his fingers, making it flash in Ben's eyes.

"How come you want to die in my territory?" he asked in Spanish.

Ben didn't allow himself to squint. "Nobody dies here but you."

The kid regarded him. "You Chicano?"

Ben shook his head. "Apache."

Into those hard eyes there came a sudden glint of respect. The kid whose ears Ben had nearly pulled off lowered his hands, looking at Ben suspiciously. There was blood trailing out of his ears. "What are you doing here?"

"Looking for answers."

"Answers to what?"

"Questions I have."

"Here's your answer," the tall kid said, and plunged forward with the knife.

Ben sidestepped, grabbed his wrist, and spun him around. It was an easy move, something taught the first week at the Native American Law Enforcement Academy in New Mexico. He pressed the kid's hand up hard between his shoulder blades. The knife dropped to the sidewalk.

"Should I break it," Ben growled into his ear, "or just tear it all the way off?"

The kid squealed. Ben pushed his hand up until his fingers were tickling the back of his neck. Ligaments popped in his shoulder. He screamed.

The other kid went down, grappling for the knife. Ben pressed a foot down on his hand, crushing it against the cement with the heel of his snakeskin boot. The kid cried out. By now the short one had gotten to his feet, holding his throat with both hands. His lips were blue. He turned in a clumsy circle and staggered away. He tripped over the fallen tricycle and went sprawling.

The little children laughed and cheered.

Ben eased up on the kid's arm slightly. "Now you and me are going to have a little talk," he said.

The kid nodded.

By afternoon Calvin Steeples was roaring drunk. How it had happened was a mystery. Many things were a mystery to him now.

Like how he had made so many friends in such a short time.

"Luxury!" someone screamed in the backseat. A brown paper bag crackled. Liquid gurgled down someone's throat. "Fucking luxury, man!"

Six hearty voices shouted agreement. The radio blasted soul tunes. The air conditioner hummed.

The tires squealed.

"Missed him," someone else cried. An electric window was slid down. Heads leaned out, shouting and laughing.

Calvin glanced in the rearview mirror, trying to place names with faces. The guy with the bald head was Dewey. The two leaning out the back window were Don and Eddie, the brothers. The one drinking out of the bottle in the bag was Hector.

Beside Calvin, riding shotgun in the big white Cadillac, were Otis and Chuckles. Otis was reaching behind him for the bag, wrenching it out of Hector's hands. A small fight ensued. Chuckles was busy puking on the floor.

It was all a great mystery.

He had requested a Cadillac at the Avis desk at O'Hare because, first of all, he had never owned a Cadillac in his life, and second of all, because Luke had given him enough money after he signed the contract to *buy* a Cadillac if he wanted to. He figured Luke had in mind that a lot of cash was going to be needed to make people open up and talk to him here. Luke was wrong. All it had taken was the Cadillac and seven bottles of Ten High. He had stopped at the curb on Thornton Street, where these six gentlemen were sharing a bottle of Thunderbird, and asked if they could help him with some information.

"Sure, brother," the man who turned out to be Hector had said. "I see you have air-conditioning on this hot day. Mind if I sit inside? This old man can't cope with the heat like he used to."

Somehow they all got in. They introduced themselves. They admired the leather upholstery. They inspected the electronic instrument panel. They requested a test drive and suggested Thornton Street Liquors as a possible destination. They had a fisherman's crafty gleam in their yellowed and aged eyes; they knew they had landed a sucker.

Now Calvin looked blearily down at the bottle nestled between his legs. An inch or two was left. He was supposed to be asking questions about crime in Chicago. He was supposed to be playing detective. He was supposed to be putting together an intelligence report for Luke. He was not supposed to be getting plastered with a carload of geriatric winos.

When he looked up, he saw a red Ford coming at him head-on. For a confused moment he thought he was back in England, where he had been stationed for a year in the Air Force. For a moment he thought the Limey coming at him had gone nuts.

"*Shit*!!!" six voices screamed in unison.

A brown hand flashed out of the group and jerked Calvin's steering wheel hard to the right. Tires barked. The red Ford sped past, honking, waving fists. The phrase "Dumb motherfucker" roared out.

"This is crazy," Calvin said. He veered over to the curb. He bounced up over the curb. He took out a stop sign. It groaned under the car, pulling things loose. The exhaust system took on new, deeper tones.

"What you stopping for, man?" Hector leaned forward to ask in his old man's gravelly voice. Chuckles continued to barf noisily on the litter of empty bottles on the floor. The smell of digested liquor floated in the car like a fog.

Calvin rested his forehead on the steering wheel. "I picked you guys up to answer some questions," he said over the noise of the radio. "Not for this."

"You worried about the cops, brother? Hell, no sweat. The cops don't come down to the South Side anymore. It's a free ride for everybody."

"They don't?" Calvin's forehead knotted with puzzlement. It came to him in a foggy sort of way that this was what he'd been after. "Why not?"

"Payoffs, man. The fuzz is being paid to stay out."

"Yeah? By who?"

"Who knows?"

"Then how do you know they're being paid off?"

"Everybody knows, man. Why else would people be getting murdered and stuff, and the cops don't even show up? Hell, the TV's full of it. Murder. Arson. Rape. Torture."

Calvin blinked. "Torture?"

Hector prodded his shoulder with two thick fingers. "Drive, brother. I'll show you something you ain't never seen before."

"What?"

"Just drive."

He drove. The Cadillac lumbered down off the curb like a wounded dinosaur. A hubcap popped loose and rolled away, winking in the sunlight. Things clunked underneath as he found the pavement and headed south on Henning. Now the car was developing a bothersome rattle somewhere under the hood. Calvin made a note to tell Avis about this.

He looked in the rearview mirror and saw Hector's wrinkled face there. Suddenly the man had grown very sober.

"How far?" Calvin asked him.

"To 152nd. Turn left there."

"Okay." Calvin drove, after a fashion. The world swam in and out of focus. His stomach lurched at each bump in the potholed street. When he came to 152nd Street, he swung left. Now everyone had grown quiet. They looked out the tinted windows anxiously.

And it was different here, Calvin noticed. The crumbling tenements were the same, but the streets were somehow different. It struck him then that there were no people here. A dilapidated easy chair lay on its side on the curb, as if dropped there from above. The burned-out carcass of a car sat crossways on the street. Multicolored piles of discarded clothes ruffled in the slight afternoon breeze. The windows here were broken, gaping eyes.

It was a ghost slum.

"Spooky," the man named Dewey said. He reached across the seat and turned the radio off. Chuckles raised himself up in the silence, observed things for a moment, groaned, then slumped down again. He made noises. The dry heaves had him in their clutches.

"Over there, on the right," Hector said, pointing. "The redbrick building."

Calvin drew up beside it and stopped. It occurred to him that the IRS had been here, that this is what was left after they got through with you. But no, that couldn't be right. Something even more devious had been at work here.

He glanced up and saw a face in a window. The shade was quickly pulled down. Not a ghost slum, then. Just a very eerie place.

They got out. Chuckles stayed behind. Calvin put his bottle on the hood as he skirted the car. Someone else— Don, he thought—picked it up and drained it in three swallows, then pitched it high into the air. It arced down and shattered on the silent street, spraying glass to both curbs.

No response. The breeze seemed to groan past these decaying buildings, hooting through the fire escapes, whispering along the tufts of dead grass in the cracks of the sidewalks. Calvin shook his head to clear it. Where the hell were all the people? The next block looked just as dead.

"Up here," Hector said, going up the steps. Calvin followed him. At the top, double doors stood propped open with chunks of cement block. He could see a dark hallway receding beyond that. There were dropped articles of clothing in there too. A white high-heeled shoe had been left in the middle of the floor. To the right, someone's belt lay coiled like a sleeping snake. A sagging mattress was upended against one wall.

"They gone now, most of them," Hector said. "They got the message."

They went inside. The light was dim in there, filtered through grimy, barred windows. It was muggy and hot, like an old attic. The smell of sour diapers hung in the air, but it was an old smell, fading now. Below that was just the slightest hint of something dead.

"Down this hallway," Hector said. Calvin stuck close to him. They walked single file—Hector, Calvin Steeples, Dewey, Otis, Don, and Eddie—bent slightly at the waist, walking on tiptoe like criminals. Occasionally one would thud against a wall and be quickly shushed by the others. The threadbare carpet muffled their footfalls.

There was probably no need to be quiet, Calvin knew, but he wanted to be quiet all the same. This was the kind of ghost building where things moved in the dark, where shadows in human shape materialized out of nowhere, where things slithered and bumped when you weren't looking. It reminded Calvin of the condemned and boarded-up tenements of Watts, where he had played as a child against his mother's orders. He felt a trembling sort of apprehension steal over him. Sweat began to trickle down his face. What had Hector brought him here to see?

Hector stopped, indicating a door a few paces ahead. "This is the room, I think. I heard about it from one of the people who was moving out. I had to see for myself, dumb-ass that I is. I swore I'd never come back here. If I wasn't drunk off my ass, I wouldn't."

He went to the door with Calvin and the rest on his

heels. It was already open a crack. He motioned for Calvin to step ahead.

"The cops was called," he said. "Maybe a dozen times. Nothing."

Calvin touched the door. It drifted open on creaking hinges. The smell of putrefaction wafted out. Whatever was dead, was dead in here.

He stuck his head inside. It was a run-down apartment. The window shades were down. In the hot gloom he could see a battered sofa with faded doilies on the arms, a set of lumpy-looking chairs, a coffee table with knickknacks on it. It looked like a place where an old person would live. There was a bookshelf on one wall with small flower vases on it. The flowers were drooped and dying. Nothing seemed out of place. Nothing seemed unusual.

Except the smell.

He stepped inside. The others remained crammed in the doorway, looking around with huge eyes. Otis was holding his nose.

"In the other room," Hector whispered. "The bedroom."

Calvin went past the coffee table to an open doorway on the right. Sweat stung his eyes, and he brushed it away. Now he could hear something unusual as well. He could hear the buzzing of lots of flies.

He took a long breath, held it, and stepped through the doorway.

The man had been dead perhaps five days. Stark naked, he had been hung by the thumbs with a length of electrical cord running up to a light fixture in the high ceiling. His head lolled back against his shoulder blades. His eyes were frozen open in a horrified, eternal stare. There was a length of white tape over his mouth. Flies crawled on him.

Calvin felt his stomach lurch. He covered his mouth with his hands.

The old man's feet had been sawed off. They were

neatly parked together under the bed, like tomorrow's shoes. Thick liquid dripped from his stumps. The floor was black with dry blood. There was a spray of it on the walls, as if the man had kicked a lot after his feet were gone. The flies were busy with that too.

Calvin stepped closer. Something had been hung around his neck, a small placard on a string. Squinting in the dim light, Calvin read the neatly typewritten words: GET OUT NOW.

He turned and stumbled into the other room.

"See what I mean?" Hector whispered.

Calvin nodded. "Looks like something the Mafia would do." He went out into the hallway and eased the door shut behind himself. "Is that what's been going on here? Organized crime? Gangland stuff?"

Hector rolled his eyes. "Nobody knows. They only knows that they is supposed to get out. And they *is*, brother. They is getting out."

"Landlords, then?"

"Ain't no landlord in the world *that* mean. No, the landlords here are small-time dudes. Sure, they be rich compared to us, but Howard Hughes they ain't. They don't have enough money to hire somebody to do what was done here, and other places."

Calvin frowned. "There's more?"

Hector nodded, his dark face full of grim lines. "About two miles this way, and two miles that way." He made broad sketches in the air. "As far as you can see in either direction, the people is moving out. They been scared out. Ain't no Mafia gonna do that. The Mafia don't pick on poor people. We ain't shit to them. Nope, ain't no Mafia doing this."

"Who, then?"

Hector shook his old head sadly. "Nobody knows, man. Nobody knows."

• • •

Larry Vandevere didn't know, either.

He was lying on his side on a motel bed with his hands tied behind his back. His ankles had been roped together. A short length of twine stretched behind him from his hands to his feet, drawing them toward each other, holding him in a backward fetal position. The heels of his shoes scraped his knuckles.

There was a black cloth bag over his head. It was hard to breath through, but he was getting used to it. Rudy and the other guy had slipped it over him as soon as they put him in the Learjet, as if they were afraid he would look out the Learjet's porthole windows and see something incriminating down below. The flight had lasted three and a half hours, by his reckoning. Afterward he had been hustled off the plane, stuck in another trunk (this one noticeably smaller than the Lincoln's had been), shuttled for an interminably long and bouncy time, and brought to this motel. He knew it was a motel because he could hear the sound of a TV playing in an adjacent room, and because it smelled like a motel, all deodorized and fresh. Besides, a little light filtered through the bag, and he could make out the shape of another large bed and a framed painting on one wall. Rudy had used the toilet, and it flushed like something in a bus station.

Motel, all right. But where?

He squirmed against the ropes, no longer trying to break free. That had proven useless hours ago and had worn him out for nothing. He was simply trying to find some sort of comfortable position.

Neither Rudy nor the other man had bothered to turn on the air conditioner before they left, and it was unsufferably hot in there, had been unsufferably hot for the last twelve hours.

Twelve hours? Twenty-four? Larry's instinctive sense

of time was being destroyed in this bag, had shorted out in this suffocating little hell. His clothes, the brown slacks and white shirt he had been wearing since picking up Missy and leaving Chicago four days ago, had become a part of him, were stuck to his body like warm glue. And his nose itched—dear God, his nose itched like crazy. He had been rubbing it raw inside the bag, and if once, just once, he could get his hands free, he would spend the first hour of his freedom using his fingernails to scratch the itch that had built on his nose like a sore and was now threatening to extinguish his sanity.

He flopped on the bed. Springs squeaked mutedly. A neighboring TV sent voices through the walls. He forced himself to stop flopping, knowing he was near the edge of the bed and would soon tumble off onto the carpet. That wouldn't improve things at all.

He tried to think rationally. He had been there for hours, perhaps a day. What did they have in mind, Rudy and the other guy? To let him die here? A three-and-a-half-hour flight for that?

Surely not. Something was cooking; brains were thinking out there. Larry Vandevere was a problem. He was a problem that would have to be handled. If they wanted Larry Vandevere dead, they would have killed him on the spot, at that mom-and-pop gas station in Arizona, that Higgery place so near to where Luke Simpson kept himself these days. They would have iced him, as the TV shows liked to say. They would have iced Larry Vandevere on the spot.

But they hadn't iced him.

And Missy had gotten away.

He didn't know how she had done it, but it made his heart beat a little bit easier to think she had. Already he had replayed his memory of those rapid-fire events over and over in his mind, trying to figure out what happened, trying to see things he hadn't been able to see.

Rudy and his pal had thrown him in the trunk of the Lincoln. Slam, the light went out. Larry had pounded on the trunk, hurt his hands, then stopped to listen. Rudy had said something. The other had answered. There were footsteps receding on the gravel. A car roared; Larry's own car roared from an idle to berserk in the space of a second, and then faded away as if someone—a particularly anxious race driver, perhaps—had jumped in and driven off.

Missy? Impossible. She didn't know how to drive.

But then again, how hard was it to learn? Especially when your life's hanging on the line?

He nodded to himself inside the bag. Sure. She had gotten away. Somehow she had gotten away.

Maybe even made it to Luke's. *Probably* even made it to Luke's. Higgery was the last stop on the way to *that* remote place.

But damn, it was all guesswork.

The Lincoln had charged off, as if following. Larry bounced in the trunk, smelling exhaust, straining to hear. Things bumped. Things crashed. The car lurched sideways again and again. It seemed to gain on the Chrysler, then lose it. Rudy and his shady friend up front shouted things at each other. Wind pummeled through the open windows, noisy even in the trunk. Tires squealed. And then, and then . . .

Quiet. Larry had raised his head from the floor of the trunk, trying to hear over the pounding of his heart. Sweat burned in his eyes. They had stopped. There was no other sound, except maybe a distant bird chattering. Then Rudy shouted.

"*Come on out, girl!*"

Of course. It had been Missy they were chasing. That

crazy, wacky, wonderful little girl of his had led them on a high-speed chase. Not bad for a nine-year-old kid.

A little bit later the shooting started.

A far-off firecracker noise. Pop. Then, later, another pop. One more pop and glass broke. Another pop and one of the men gasped. Another pop and pretty soon the car shifted as people got in.

A long time driving, then.

And later, the deal with the flying motorcycle. No other way to explain it. A big buzzing motorcycle on wings. Had to be. It went up, it went down, it was all around. It shot at them. But when the shotgun started going off, it began sounding like a used-up Honda with a few bad cylinders. Then it went away.

One of Luke's boys? Some kind of ultralight aircraft?

Larry gritted his teeth inside the bag. There was no way to know for sure. And maybe Missy hadn't gotten away at all. Maybe one of those firecracker pops had gotten her, and she was dead now on the desert. That thought brought a surge of terrible despair. What if the whole frantic trip had been for nothing? Questions. His head ached with them. Too many questions that might never be answered.

Keys rattled in a lock. Larry jerked up on the bed, turning his head to catch the sound. The door swung open, letting in the brief noise of traffic outside. The door thudded shut. Feet came across the carpet.

"Okay, hero," someone said. "Time to go."

Chapter 7

Jake O'Bannion was beginning to see things from a new perspective.

As a thirty-year veteran of the New York City Police Department, he had made thousands of arrests, put thousands of people in temporary lockup, seen thousands of criminals make their slow progress through the court system to spend time in prison, thanks to him. But he had never done time in the lockup himself.

Things looked weird from in here. In here, things looked the way things probably looked to a monkey behind bars in a zoo. The world had become suddenly crowded and crazy, too small to survive in. He was in a cage made of bars and wires. If he could pace it off, he would find that it measured fourteen feet by fourteen feet. Here in the first sublevel of the Chicago metro police headquarters, there were six of these cages facing each other, with narrow aisles in between for the policemen to walk as they dragged new internees in. That was one of the crazy things here, Jake had noticed as the hours passed: They kept bringing people in, but no one ever seemed to leave.

And there were several other crazy things here. The general noise level was one. It sounded like an echoing gymnasium full of high-school kids. Men shouted at each other, shoved each other, tried to find space to stand or sit. Fights broke out at least once every fifteen minutes, causing the duty officer to rush over and bang the bars with his nightstick. Somewhere, in one of the other cages, a man was screaming and weeping in garbled Spanish. To Jake's immediate left, an old man had gone to sleep on his feet, leaning up against the bars, and was drooling down his shirt. The cement floor was slick with spit and some brazen bastard's urine. The whole place stank like an outhouse. Crazy.

Jake looked at his wrist for the fiftieth time since being stuck in here. There was nothing there but a ring of paleness on the suntanned skin of his arm to remind him that they had seized his watch, his wallet, his keys, and his belt when they put him in there. His fingertips were stained with black ink from the fingerprinting. They had taken his crutches, which were considered possible weapons. They had taken his St. Christopher medal to keep him from hanging himself. Had his balls not been attached, he supposed they would have taken them too.

Yet he understood the reasoning behind all of this. It was all very necessary. But to do this to a retired *cop*, for Chrissake? A thirty-year man like himself?

The steel door to the subfloor clanged open. Another guest was escorted in. A hundred voices shouted at the sweaty, uniformed cop, demanding release, demanding lawyers, threatening to take a piece of his ass if he didn't let them out. He shoved the man in a cell and heaved the door shut. He turned and stalked past Jake's cell. Their eyes met for a moment. He had cop's eyes, Jake realized with a sudden burst of recognition. The dead, flat eyes of a cop who has worked too many hours, been paid too little, seen too much to give a shit anymore. He also had a red lightning bolt of a scar jagging across his right cheek. Fresh one too. Somebody had hooked him a good one there with a not very sharp object. Jake could sympathize. He carried his own scar, a pink dimple below his navel, where a punk's .25 auto had caught him point-blank. The docs had used six feet of number-eight nylon to stitch his bladder back together.

"Howdy," Jake mumbled.

Surprisingly the cop nodded before walking on. But he did walk on, and that left Jake with the noise and the heat and the standing room only of Chicago's main lockup.

Minutes passed. Jake checked his wrist, grimaced, shook his head. He had been offered the customary one phone call but had refused it. No one to call, really. This was his own fuck-up, and he would deal with it alone. His leg hurt like hell, a big extra heartbeat below his knee. His head was better, though. It only hurt when he breathed.

The door clanged open. The clamor died down momentarily. A tired-looking cop stepped in with a piece of paper in his hand. "O'Bannion?" he called out.

People shouted. Hands waved. Men climbed the cages and screamed.

The duty officer checked a roster and led the officer to Jake's cage. He pointed Jake out and opened the door. Jake fought his way out, hopping on his one good leg.

"This way, O'Bannion."

They went through the steel door, up a flight of stairs. Jake breathed the air of freedom, grateful for it. At the top they went left, to the out-processing desk. Jake's belongings were dumped out of a manila envelope for him to inspect and sign for. His crutches were returned. He put his belt back on, his St. Christopher, and checked his wallet for the fifteen-hundred dollars Luke had given him. All there. The cop led him by the elbow to the big double front doors, released him, and turned away.

"That's it?" Jake said.

The cop turned back. "If it wasn't, you wouldn't be up here."

Jake shrugged to himself. It was all pretty clear. The cabbie had decided not to file a complaint. Probably knew he didn't have much of a case. Or more likely, didn't want to sacrifice hours, maybe days, of his time pursuing this thing in the tangled mess of the courts. Smart guy—for a dumb-ass.

Jake went outside. Chicago's foul air greeted him, stinking of bus exhaust but inestimably better than the air down below. He worked his way down the shallow stone steps, hurrying at first, then slowing as he realized that it was late afternoon and he had accomplished nothing so far. He was here to talk to the police. Why be going down these steps when the police were back there?

Someone drew up beside him. He glanced over and saw the same tired eyes and fresh facial scar he had seen on the cop walking through the lockup. Then the cop hurried past, his shoes slapping on the limestone steps.

"Hey, buddy," Jake shouted. "Wait up."

The cop turned. Jake manuevered downward, puffing now from the exertion of working these damn extra arms. He caught up to the cop and extended a hand.

"O'Bannion, NYPD, retired. Excuse the lumber, but I caught some double-ought on my last bust, the day before I got the gold watch. Puerto Rican dopers, and damn crazy ones." He indicated his leg. "Might never walk again, but that's the way she goes, huh? We all have our scars to bear."

The cop smiled and caught his hand. "Roberts. Weren't you downstairs?"

"Misunderstanding. I clobbered a purse snatcher with one of my wooden legs here, and they thought I was the perp. The old lady was too hysterical to get her shit straight. Soon as she did, I was out. She got her purse out of the deal, anyway. I got to tour your facilities."

The cop named Roberts laughed. "Hell of a way to see Chicago. What brings you here?"

"I wanted to see old friends before I hit the beaches in Miami. Do you know a Freddie O' Reilly? He's with you guys now."

Roberts shook his head. "Can't say as I do."

"Oh, he's on the Morton Grove force, but that wouldn't be the same, would it? Sort of like a Manhattan cop looking for a friend in Queens. We can't all know each other, can we?"

"With two thousand of us working in metro alone, I guess we can't."

"How about Larry Vandevere, then? Know where I might find him?"

"Vandevere?" Roberts grinned uneasily. "You know him?"

"Sure do. I'm practically like a grandfather to his daughter Missy."

"Well." Roberts looked back up at the building. He stared out across the street, then up at the hazy gray sky. He touched Jake's elbow, motioning for him to follow, and went down the steps to the sidewalk. There he opened the door to his patrol car and got in.

Jake lumbered after him. "Are we going for a ride?" he asked as he sat inside.

Roberts shook his head. "No, I just wanted to be away from all the ears up there." His expression became grave. "I'll be honest with you, O'Bannion. I don't know what's happened to Larry Vandevere. I used to be good friends with him back a few years ago. Poker every Friday with him and the boys, things like that. Then we sort of drifted away. You know how that happens when you're working different shifts all the time. But I'd still see him every once in a while, pass him in the halls and say hi. But now he's gone. I asked somebody if he'd quit, and they told me I ought to mind my own business. I asked the chief whatever had happened to Vandevere, and he acted like he didn't know who I was talking about. Somebody said he got transferred. But I don't think that's all there is to it.''

Jake hiked an eyebrow. "How come?"

Roberts sighed. "You were a cop, O'Bannion. Did you ever get the feeling something wasn't quite kosher in the department? People got closemouthed all of a sudden? You turned in arrest reports and they wound up missing? You locked up bad guys, and suddenly they were let out, the charges dropped, everything covered up?"

"Not in my precinct," Jake said. "We had a good crew."

"Well, something's wrong here. Something's deeply wrong. It's like a two-mile section at the bottom of the South Side has dropped off the planet. I used to be dispatched to that area five, maybe six times a day. We had gang fights, robberies, murders, rapes—the usual. Then, two weeks ago, nothing. The streets from about 140th to 164th have suddenly become crime-free. From Loeser to Hasselman Streets east and west, same thing. On a big chunk of the South Side map, crime doesn't exist anymore. And if you happen to be cruising the area and catch something going down, the perp walks out of the lockup an hour later, scot-free. You go to check his paper, and the file is missing. You ask the chief about it, and the next thing you know, you're out getting cats out of old ladies' trees clear up in Skokie.''

He took off his hat and ran a hand through his hair. "Me, I'm not stupid. If they want me out of that area, I'm staying out. You don't need to beat me over the head with a stick before I get the message. But Larry—you know how he is. Overachiever. Super-snooper. Not one to follow orders if the orders don't make sense. He smelled the same rat I'm smelling, got noisy about it, so they transferred him, I guess. At least I hope that's what they did with him. The way things are here, they might have done something worse.''

Jake nodded. Something worse was exactly what they did. They chased him and his daughter halfway across the country, kidnapped him, and tried to get his daughter.

''Any idea who's behind it?'' Jake asked.

Roberts put his hat back on, shrugging. ''It's probably best not to know these things, but if you want my gut reaction, I'd say the mob's involved. I don't see any other way to explain it.'' He chuckled miserably. ''Only thing is, why would they want to keep us out of *that* rotten area? What have they got to gain? A corner on the roach market?''

''I don't know,'' Jake said. ''It depends on who's running the show. How does the local mob work here?''

''Same as everywhere, I guess. You've got three or four families, each with their own specialty and their own turf. But they're pretty quiet, all in all. You won't find much of that New York stuff going on here, the mass murders and all. It's not the Midwestern style. Here, they operate with more finesse.''

''So who's in charge? The headman, I mean. The kingpin.''

Roberts thought about it. ''Probably Mel Corsica right now. Yeah, Corsica would be your man.''

''Where do I find him?''

''You?'' Roberts laughed. ''People don't find Mel Corsica. He finds them. And you better pray he never goes looking for you.''

''I'm serious,'' Jake said. ''Where does he live?''

''On the lakefront, in the Hastings Park area, if you must know. The biggest, swankiest mansion on the beach. It's another area we stay away from. We don't bother him, and he doesn't bother us. We coexist on terms of mutual hostility.''

"Hastings Park, huh?" Jake smiled. "Okay, Roberts. Thanks.''

He started to get out, then felt Roberts's hand on his elbow. He turned. "Yeah?"

Roberts's face was grave again. "I hope you can find Larry," he said. "But if it means talking to Mel Corsica, I suggest you let the matter drop. Corsica eats small fry like us for breakfast. He eats bigger fry for lunch. You could disappear faster than Larry did.''

"Don't worry," Jake said. "I don't plan on talking to him.''

Roberts looked relieved. "Good. I'd hate to see a crippled veteran like you start throwing accusations around and wind up dead.''

"Not me," Jake said. He grinned. "I leave stuff like that for my boss.''

Larry Vandevere found his new accommodations pleasant compared to the old ones. Instead of a bed he had a deck chair; instead of a motel he had a boat.

Quite bizarre, he was thinking. Pleasant but decidedly bizarre.

Country and western music was playing below, drifting up to him from the lower deck of the boat. Johnny Paycheck was singing about some old gal he'd known in Memphis. The boat sped across mildly choppy water, bucking heavily up and down, its engines a deep, powerful thrum. To Larry it sounded like a yacht. He had never been on a yacht before, never been close to one, really. But even with the bag over his head and his arms tied to the deck chair, he knew he was on a yacht.

They had been under way for about ten minutes. After being untied and taken out of the motel, he had been stuck in a trunk again, driven over smooth streets for a half an hour, yanked out and set on his feet, and marched across a wooden pier to the waiting ladder of this boat. A little urging had got him to climb up it. Even through the bag he had smelled the clean, cool air blowing off the water. He had heard the gentle slap of waves against a wooden hull. He had made one final, futile break for freedom before this water could cut him off from land and rescue, had swung blindly out and hit someone, and for his trouble he had been blasted squarely on the nose with what had to be the world's largest fist. He had dropped like a rock.

He woke up strapped to this chair with the wind flapping the bag against his face. But he knew where he was.

Lake Michigan. He had lived in Chicago too long not to know the sound of it and the smell of it. He could almost see the broad, gray-blue expanse of water stretching to the horizon in front of him, and the jutting high rises of downtown Chicago sticking up from the naked shoreline like distant gray teeth.

They had brought him home.

The engines throttled down to a deep, resonant hum, and the boat began to slow. Larry cocked his head this way and that, trying to pick up sounds that would help identify where they were landing, but the music blocked everything. Someone clopped over to him on the wooden deck and untied his arms. He was hoisted to his feet.

"Get moving."

Hands prodded him forward. He walked hesitantly, searching for solid footing with his toes, stepping like a blind man. It came to him that they had not landed anywhere, that around them lay the restless waters of Lake Michigan and nothing more; he was about to be walked to the edge of the deck and be shoved overboard. It would make sense, in a way. Bothersome Larry Vandevere would no longer be a problem.

But surely they wouldn't bring him this far just to drown him. That wouldn't make sense.

"Turn around."

He turned.

"There's a ladder behind you. Walk down it."

He shuffled backward. The deck dropped off to nothing. He searched with his foot and found a step. He manuevered downward. Hands were waiting at the bottom to take his elbows. He was guided across a wooden pier and down several steps. At the bottom his feet encountered cement.

He was urged on. After a few steps the cement became sand. He bumped into something, cracking his shins.

"Sit."

His hands fumbled over some kind of padded seat. He reached farther and encountered hard plastic.

"It's a golf cart, dumb-ass, not an electric chair. *Sit!*"

He sat in it. The other person went around to the other side and settled himself in. The cart jumped forward with an electric whine. They rattled over lumpy ground.

"Okay," the man said after a minute. "The boat's out of sight. You can take the hood off."

Larry reached up and worked on the drawstring that was knotted around his neck. When it was loose, he tore the bag off his head. Light flooded his eyes.

"If you try to hit me again, I'll tear your head off, Vandevere. You understand me?"

Squinting, Larry nodded. The man sitting beside him in the driver's seat of the cart looked big enough, and mean enough, to do it. There was a Uzi strapped casually over his chest. He had to weigh in at fully three hundred pounds, of which not much was wasted on fat. He was wearing a black shirt with a red collar, and red pants. Beneath curly brown hair was a long face with a big twisted hook of a nose.

Herman Munster, Larry thought dazedly. *I am riding in a golf cart with Herman Munster.*

He took in the scenery around him. A pale spot of sun hung in the gray western sky, indicating late afternoon. They were driving over sandy terrain dotted with clumps of weeds. To the left a narrow, curving shoreline met the deeper gray of the lake. Ahead, about a hundred yards away, the sand became a rolling expanse of well-tended grass. At the fringe of that stood a tall wrought-iron fence topped with three twists of barbed wire. There seemed to be a guardhouse of sorts at the gate. The gate itself opened on a broad concrete drive, which led to a house.

Larry stared at it. *House* was a poor word for this imposing structure. Built of massive white stone blocks, it rose to the sky in six rambling stories, eclipsing half of the eastern horizon. He counted thirty windows on this side alone before he gave up. There were tall stone spires bulking up at each end, topped with flagpoles. Huge red and black flags rustled in the damp lake breeze. Manicured hedges ran around its perimeter. The flat rectangle of a tennis court lay to the left; to the right was a putting green. The place had, to Larry's amazed eyes, the look of a grand European hotel.

The man driving the cart glanced at Larry as he drove. "Nice joint, eh?"

Larry snorted. "It'll do."

"I suppose you've seen better."

"Every day."

"Smart-ass."

They drove to the guardhouse and stopped. The man standing inside looked down at them, nodded, and pressed a button on a console mounted on the wall. The gates clanked open. He was also carrying an Uzi and wearing a black shirt with a red collar, and through the guardhouse window Larry could see the waistband of his red pants. Someone walking across the lawn carrying a rake was also dressed this way, right down to the Uzi on a strap.

How swift, Larry thought. The guys here all dress like pizza delivery boys.

They drove through. At the end of the driveway an overhanging porch jutted out, its stone carapace supported by the reaching hands of tall white statues. Pink roses sprouted at their feet in pristine symmetry. Larry noticed that they were fake flowers. Odd.

The cart stopped. "Out here," the big man said.

Larry got out. He dropped the bag on the seat, glad to be rid of it at last. "What now?"

The big man, Herman Munster, picked it up and smiled at him. "Back in the bag, asshole. Now."

Groaning, Larry fitted it back over his head. It smelled like dry spit. He knotted it loosely around his throat and stood waiting, blind once again.

The springs on the cart squeaked. "Okay, asshole, this way."

He was jerked forward by the elbow, up two steps. The massive front door swung open on well-oiled hinges. He stepped through onto thickly padded carpet.

"Now just stay with me and keep your mouth shut, dipshit. In here you do as you're told."

He was led through the house. As he walked he tried to form some kind of mental map, noting the rights and lefts, the jaunts down hallways, the trips up stairs. If he ever broke away from Herman here and managed to get the bag off his head again, it would be nice to know the way out. But it soon became impossible, and he gave up. The house was just too big.

"Okay, hold it right here."

He stopped.

Herman knocked on a door. A second later a female voice crackled through an intercom. "Yes?"

"Manning here. I have the special project."

Ah, Manning, Larry thought. Not Herman, after all.

"Step through."

The door squeaked. Larry had the impression that it had slid sideways, like a door on *Star Trek*. Missy was crazy about that show.

They went on. The floor here was hard and slick. The air smelled like a hospital, full of antiseptics. Through the bag he saw the bright bars of fluorescent lights overhead. They turned right and stopped again.

"That's him?" a woman said.

"In the flesh."

"I'll announce you."

Another door squeaked, and she was gone. Ten seconds later it squeaked again. "Okay," she said. A sheaf of what felt like tissue paper was thrust into Larry's hands. "Put these on."

"Aw, cripes," Manning said. "I get sick of this shit."

Larry unfolded the sheaf, confused. It was just a big sheet of thin paper with a hole in the middle.

"Over your head," the woman said to him. "Like a poncho."

Larry put the hole over his head. It was, like she had said, a poncho. He frowned inside the bag, feeling wrapped and constricted.

"All right," Manning said, "we're set."

The door squeaked. They walked through, rustling. The door squeaked shut behind them. Manning guided Larry to a chair and pushed him down.

Someone sneezed.

"Gesundheit, boss," Manning said.

"Go to hell. Get back by the door and shoot this guy if he stands up. And next time wash your hair before you dare come in here."

"Right, boss."

"Vandevere!"

Larry cocked his head.

"You move out of that chair and Manning will shoot you deader than dogshit. *Comprende*?"

Larry shrugged. "Who are you?"

"None of your fucking beeswax who I am. Sit still and listen. Did you get a look at my mansion when you drove up here?"

Manning spoke up. "Yeah, I showed him."

"Shut up. I asked Vandevere. Just stand there and keep your mouth shut, goddammit, or I'll hire somebody who will. Vandevere!"

Jesus, Larry thought. What a grouch. He nodded to signal he had heard.

The man sneezed again. He groaned. "Fucking summertime. You saw my place, right? You saw what money can build. I've got more money in loose change than you've got in the bank." He sneezed. and cursed. "Shit! Don't wiggle around so much, Vandevere, you're filling up the air."

He blew his nose. He sniffed. "I have invested millions of dollars in payoffs and bribes, Vandevere. I have purchased every politician, newsman, and police official who would hold still long enough to have his pockets filled. I have worked methodically and patiently in order to achieve my goal. Then you come along and decide to fuck me up."

He sneezed again. He wheezed and cursed. Something clicked, and a distant fan hummed. Medicinal-smelling air moved through the room.

"Ugh. Jesus. I'd burn every flower and weed in the world if I could. Vandevere, were you or were you not approached by one of my people at about the time you began making waves?" He sneezed. "Shit! Were you or were you not offered a large sum of money to play along?"

"I was."

"Are you one of those TV cops who's so goddamn

honest, he won't accept a simple bribe? Have I actually run across an honest man?"

"Looks that way."

"*Achoo!* Shit! Bullshit! Every man has his price. Your own friends on the force have turned against you. People you trusted for years are in my pocket, and they don't even know who I am. Your own people chased you all the way to Arizona so that I might have this interview with you, and they don't even know who I am. I'm easy money to them and nothing more. You can be bought, Vandevere. It's simply a matter of negotiating the right price."

"And if I refuse?"

"Then you'll force me to violate a personal principle. All my life I have worked within the framework of anonymous friendly persuasion to achieve my goals. Not once have I been reduced to murdering a cop. There are little people that get in the way, I'll admit, and sometimes these must be given special handling. But we're talking about peasants, unimportant baggage whose lives have no more worth than a blade of grass. I will not give you the satisfaction of causing me to commit a federal offense. You will be bought, Larry Vandevere, one way or another. *Achoo!* Shit! Manning! I want you to shave your head next time! Do you hear me?"

Across the room, Manning sighed. "Yes, boss."

"Think of it! Two square miles of Chicago's most blighted section, turned into a glistening architectural masterpiece. High-rise offices and condominiums, monuments of steel and glass, sparkling fountains, happy people. Dust into diamonds. Tenements into condos."

"Sure," Larry said. "And the people who live there now can just go to hell."

"Yes! Yes! Or back to Mexico, back to Africa! Away with all the peasants! Bit by bit we'll reclaim South Chicago from them. We'll turn their despair into our hope.

We'll show the world what can be done if we set our goals high enough. We'll make the slums into a fairyland.''

Larry shook his head, wishing he could see this man. He imagined that if he took the bag off his head now, he would be looking at a lunatic. A very rich and powerful lunatic. "The fairyland is in your head," he said.

"Dreams create reality. You'll see. You'll be with us as we create the new world.''

"Don't count on it.''

He heard the slap of a hand on a desk. "Ten thousand dollars, Mr. Vandevere. And the freedom to go back to your job.''

"No.''

"Twenty thousand.''

Larry shook his head.

"Thirty thousand. More than you make in a year.''

"No ''

"Forty, then. My final offer.''

"Eat shit.''

"Stubborn bastard. Manning, get him out of here.''

Manning marched over. "Where to?''

"Go kick the shit out of him. Work him over bad. Beat him half to death, knock a few of his teeth out. Find a rubber hose and use it. When he starts to see the light, let me know. *Achoo!* Shit! Now get out of here before I die.''

"Right, boss.''

Chapter 8

By one-thirty that night Luke was over Chicago, having
passed Calvin Steeples, Ben Sanchez, and Jake O'Bannion
in the air as they winged back toward Arizona and a good
night's sleep. By one forty-five he was in the Continental
terminal on the ground, collecting his remarkably heavy
false-bottomed Samsonite suitcase from the revolving
carousel.

By two-fifteen he was in a rented Ford Escort, heading
southeast on the JFK Expressway. A map of Chicago was
spread across the passenger seat. Occasionally he clicked
the dome light on to check his progress. A tingle of
anticipation stirred in his stomach. He had never taken on
the Mafia single-handedly before. It could prove interesting.

By three o'clock he was cruising slowly along Sheriden
Drive, looking for, as Jake had put it, the biggest fucking
mansion on the block. It was a pretty skimpy description
but would have to do. Mel Corsica lived here someplace.
Mel Corsica was the man to talk to. There would be the
simple matter of getting into his house, rousing him from
his bed, and asking him a few questions. Luke smiled as

he studied the houses slipping past. Should be a piece of cake. Mafia kingpins were famous for being nice to late-night prowlers.

He thought about Missy and how hard leaving her had been. He'd had to leave her in Tran Cao's unwilling hands. But by now Jake and the others were back, and she wouldn't feel so alone. And if things went right, they would know more about her dad tonight.

Ben had been the first to call in, early in the afternoon. What he had to report had cast fresh light on Larry's case. Ben reported that he had interviewed three extremely talkative young Hispanics and that they had admitted to being a part of the murderous crime wave overwhelming a certain large section of the South Side.

They had been paid to do it, they said. They had been paid to drive the people out.

Who by? Ben had asked them.

The cops, they said. The cops had paid them.

Then Calvin called in, sounding dead tired and not a little tipsy. "I've got the lowdown from the black side of the fence, O Great White Bwana," he had said between hiccups. "The brothers think it has to be the Mafia."

And then, much later, Jake's call came through. Mel Corsica was the man to talk to.

So much for the CIA's idea about the Russians, Luke thought. Ivan had better things to do with his time.

If the Chicago cops were paying for crime, Larry Vandevere wouldn't sit still for it. He'd blow the whistle on anyone he suspected. And if the Mafia was behind the whole thing, they would want to put a muzzle on him. If so, Mel Corsica would know. He would have all the answers. And answers were what Luke was after.

The houses were big here. They were mansions. Mighty lawns peppered with maples and weeping willows surrounded them. Lake Michigan was their backyard, where night surf glistened under the moon on a curving strand of beach, the black water stretching beyond to form a mysterious, sparkling rim on the eastern edge of the world.

Through his open window Luke could smell the water as he drove, cool and vaguely dank on this warm July night. These mansions all looked big. Fucking big, as Jake would have put it. Which one was Corsica's?

Sheriden Drive was ending, curving back west. Luke leaned out the window, squinting in the dark. Up ahead, on the left, lay the last house. And, yes, it looked big. Tall Doric columns supported a massive balcony above an equally massive porch. It was fully five stories tall, dwarfing the others he had seen.

He flipped his headlights to bright, slowing. This house was surrounded by a stone fence. A single electric wire ran above it. Floodlights mounted on poles cast harsh white light along the length of it. The entrance to the driveway was blocked by a steel gate.

He stopped the car before entering the glare of the floodlights, and killed the motor. If this wasn't a big fucking mansion, nothing was. He folded the map together and put it in the glove compartment, then reached into the backseat for the suitcase. Grunting against its weight, he laid it on the passenger seat and snapped the latches.

In the dim existing light he searched through the items he had brought from DFI's supply store. The eight-inch grappling hook with forty feet of eight-millimeter line he stuck under the seat—the stone fence was barely seven feet tall, and no need for that. Ditto for the insulated bolt cutters and the infrared deception assembly, six three-inch mirrors mounted on an adjustable aluminum frame, packed in bulky Styrofoam for the trip. Without knowing exactly what kind of security system Corsica had, Luke had thought it wise to bring a little bit of everything. Seeing Corsica's mansion eliminated the need for virtually most of what had been brought. His security system, at least from this vantage point, seemed to consist of an electric fence and a stone wall.

Luke shook his head and smiled. With a world of super-sophisticated anti-intrusion devices available, the Mafia still relied on wires and lights and gates, just as their grandfathers had.

And without doubt, one other thing, the oldest and perhaps best security system of all: men. Someone was probably on guard.

Luke worked the false bottom free and removed the square of fiberglass insulation that would have foiled the X rays if the suitcase had happened to pass through a detector on its way into the belly of the plane, the chances of which, Luke knew, were small. Nestled against another wall of pink fiberglass was the weapon he had chosen for this little late-night break-in, a Heckler & Koch VP70Z semiautomatic.

While he preferred a wheel gun for combat situations, Luke felt that the VP70Z's capacity—nineteen rounds of nine-millimeter firepower—weighed in its favor. Although a wheel gun could be expected to reliably deliver six rounds on demand, this nine-millimeter beauty put three times that capacity in his hands, without the inherent danger and bother involved in time-consuming reloading.

Most combat situations called for the delivery of one or two shots in an encounter of perhaps two seconds' duration; tonight he had no idea how many of Corsica's men he might run into, and what kind of firefight might develop. Hopefully none.

But if things got bad, it was nice to know the H&K carried the equivalent of three revolvers.

Movement was a critical factor here too. The VP70Z had no projecting parts—not even the front sight post, which was a notched light-and-shadow ramp—and if he had to slither down a gutter pipe, it would do no good at all to leave his weapon hanging on an exposed nail or screw. It had no hammer, no thumb safety, no slide catch, no side magazine release. The gun could pass through a knot of barbed wire without hanging up. Jake thought it looked like a space gun and distrusted it. Ben hated the plastic butt. Calvin had said it looked like something Luke Skywalker might carry.

Tonight Luke Simpson trusted it with his life.

Before he hooked the black nylon holster over his chest, he removed his shirt and stuffed it under the seat and put on the black turtleneck he had brought. With the barrel of the pistol he knocked through the rented Ford's dome light and smashed the bulb. He opened the door and removed his shoes, socks, and pants, then put on skintight black stretch slacks.

A bird shrieked in the trees on Corsica's estate. Luke ducked behind the door, watching. After a moment it stopped.

He put his shoes and socks under the seat. Out of the suitcase came a black matte camouflage stick. Luke coated his face with it, his ears, his neck, his hands. Before he put it back, he painted his bare feet. He removed two more items, a galvanized pipe-expander joint and a locksmith's tool pouch, and stuck them in his pockets. That done, he closed the suitcase and put it on the backseat.

He holstered the pistol at his chest. He smoothed his hair back with his hands. His heart thudded in his chest.

He got out and closed the door.

A beep made Tran Cao jump. He spun around in his chair.

There was a brief message on the Cray's CRT screen. For fifteen hours there had been nothing but the word WORKING hanging there in dull green. Ben and Calvin and Jake had come down to take Missy off his hands (she had been fascinated at first by all the wonderful things in

Luke's underground Disneyland, but as the hours dragged by, she got bored) and now, after all these unendurable hours in the stillness, something was happening.

The Cray was telling him something.

He took his cigarette out of his mouth and leaned forward, bleary-eyed, his mouth drooping open.

KEYLIST ERROR. RE-INPUT.

His heart jumped. The Cray had been pulsing possible entry codes into the FBI mainframe at the rate of one hundred thousand per hour. Of the millions sent, all had been so utterly out of sync with the actual code that they were ignored. And now one had come so close that the mainframe had detected it as an operator error and asked for it to be rekeyed.

He had come within one or two digits of the code.

He bent over the Cray's keyboard. His swiftly moving fingers instructed it to cease its current feed. He hesitated for a moment, wondering how long it had been since the beep had come. Surely no more than ten seconds. He instructed the computer to resubmit the last two thousand codes and halt when the FBI computer initiated a response.

The Cray burped momentarily. The screen glowed.

KEYLIST ERROR. RE-INPUT.

Tran typed: PRINT KEYLIST.

The screen filled with numbers in ten-digit sequences.

Tran slapped his forehead with his open hand, scowling. Ashes sifted off his cigarette. He typed again.

PRINT KEYLIST ERROR.

The screen blanked out. These numbers shifted to the top left: 7463522

Tran grinned. "Gonna get you, you son of a bitch." He laughed. "Gonna get you after all."

He bent to his work.

The asphalt was warm and rough against the soles of

Luke's bare feet as he ran across the road and jumped for the fence.

He caught the top with his hands and pulled himself up. The holster on his chest scraped against the stones. He put a knee on the shelf and brought himself up.

On both knees, he hunched over the single wire there, examining its moorings. Simple ceramic blocks anchored in the stone, the same kind Farmer Joe used on the fence posts that kept his cows in. Luke smiled. Archaic.

He put his hands on the shelf on the other side of the wire and somersaulted down onto the grass of the other side. He shrank against the shadow of the wall and crouched there, watching.

A half-slice of moon hung in the sky, striping the nighttime-gray landscape with black shadows. The damp night breeze off the lake rustled the trees. Crickets chirped their monotonous song. Somewhere far away a dog barked, was quiet, barked again.

Luke went down on his stomach and slithered to the moon shadow of a nearby tree. He crept up against it and pressed his cheek to the trunk.

The house was dark but for a porch light burning over the front door.

He low-crawled to the next tree, moving closer to the house. The pipe fitting was a bothersome lump in his pocket against his thigh. He reached down and stuck it in his back pocket with the tool pouch.

From this point the fence stretched off to his right. He could see the silver bars of the driveway gate fifty yards away, shining whitely under the floodlights. Beyond that, the fence fell away into a shallow valley, reappearing again on a distant rise, then angling left toward the shore, where the lights ended and the sand began.

He crawled again. Nothing moved in response. The barking dog uttered a few half-hearted yelps and was still.

Luke frowned. This was too easy. Surely a man in Corsica's position couldn't afford to live under security this lax. There had to be more to it.

His answer came as he prepared to crawl to another tree. Someone farted in the dark.

Luke froze, stifling an involuntary grin. Given enough time, even the best soldier will give his position away. Luke Simpson was not alone out here in this big front yard. Somebody with a loud case of late-night gas was out here too.

He rested his chin on his hands, watching, waiting.

Something creaked directly ahead. Luke squinted. One of the trees ahead, a big maple, seemed to have an oddly shaped trunk. Luke moved his eyes slightly to the right, using his peripheral vision to see better in the dark. A man was sitting on a lawn chair under the tree. He had tipped back on the chair's rear legs and was resting against the trunk.

The chair creaked under his weight as he shifted position. He farted again, then mumbled something.

Luke nodded imperceptibly. A man trying to stay awake on a boring night shift. Either that or a dedicated gardener watching his grass grow. There was no proof so far that this was indeed Corsica's estate.

This man would provide it.

Luke crawled off to the left, out of the line of the man's sight, and angled up behind the tree where he was resting so comfortably. Standing up, he edged around the tree until he was beside him, looking down at the side of his face.

The man was humming a tune now. His heels tapped against the lawn chair's front legs as he kept time to his inner music. His eyes glistened wetly, staring at something only he could see. He seemed to be enjoying himself immensely.

On the grass beside the chair lay the dark shape of a short rifle with a long, curving magazine. An H&K MP5, Luke guessed. Everybody's new favorite, and a damn sight better than the tommy guns of olden days.

Corsica's man, of course. Certainly no gardener.

Luke bent down and gently slid the rifle backward on the grass. The man had begun to wiggle in his chair now, doing the boogie-woogie from the waist up, snapping his fingers, singing half-formed words while humming through his nose. Luke had to give him credit. It was a hell of a snappy tune. The last song he would ever sing, and a hell of a snappy tune.

He took the pipe-expander joint out of his pocket and threaded it onto the end of the barrel of the VP70Z. Now it looked like a miniature musket. He placed his left hand over the rear of the slide to keep it from actuating, knelt, and slammed the bell-shaped pipe expander hard against the man's rib cage below his arm.

At the same instant he pulled the trigger.

The entire force and sound of the blast were funneled by the expander into the newly created bullet hole in the man's body, turning him into a natural silencer while the focused concussion pulverized his lungs.

He flipped out of the chair with blood shooting out his mouth and nose in a sudden wet spray. He thumped to the ground and rolled once. Smoke puffed out of the large burned hole in his side. The chair would have crashed over, but Luke saved it.

The crickets sang their song as if nothing had happened to disturb the serenity of Corsica's estate.

Luke shrank back against the tree, cocking the VP70Z by hand.

The house remained dark but for the porch light.

Moving from tree to tree, he came to the front steps and ducked down beside the hedges there, scanning the landscape once again for signs of movement.

Nothing. He unscrewed the expander from the barrel of the pistol and put it back in his pocket. He withdrew the tool pouch from another pocket and went to the front door. Reaching up, he unscrewed the light bulb until it went out.

It took five seconds to pick the lock.

The door swung open soundlessly. Luke pocketed the tool kit and stepped inside. He shut the door, looking around.

Big place. Chandeliers, framed paintings, fancy draperies and carpets. The smell of luxury was in the air, leather furniture and good cigar smoke. In the big living room to the left, a soft blue light above the fireplace mantle illuminated a huge painting of a man with gray hair and a mustache. He was staring straight ahead with piercing brown eyes.

Corsica?

Luke smirked. Who else?

He padded down the hallway to a curving flight of stairs. Take any average mansion, and the bedrooms will be on the second floor. Up above will be guest rooms, perhaps miniature suites for important visitors. Two or three maids will be employed full-time to keep these rooms in order. In this house at least one room will be debugged and soundproofed, used for high-level meetings with other local chieftains. The dirty business of dope and prostitution will be discussed in the most elegant of surroundings.

Luke went up the steps, stepping at the edges, where they were least likely to creak. At the top he was looking down a dimly lit hallway that stretched perhaps twenty yards. There were three doors on each side. Six rooms up here, then.

Which one was the master bedroom?

Luke went down on his knees, studying the carpet. It was thick-piled, luxuriously red. That was fine. Even the world's thickest, most expensive carpet will wear with time, and this one was no exception. The pile had been trampled in a faint path to the first door on the right.

He got up and went to it. He pressed his ear to it.

Someone was snoring.

Luke eased the door open and went inside, shutting it behind himself. He probed the wall with his left hand until he found the light switch. With his right he extended the pistol.

He snapped the light on.

It was a bedroom, all right.

The ugliest, fattest woman he had ever seen in his life raised her head off the pillow. She blinked sleepily at the ceiling. She smacked her lips. The covers were pooled at her waist, and her huge naked breasts stared at Luke with their baleful brown nipples.

She sat up in bed. She looked at Luke and opened her mouth to scream.

Luke shook his head gravely.

She closed her mouth.

"Where's Corsica?" he said.

"Not here," she squeaked.

"I know that. Where?"

Slowly, as if in a dream, she covered herself up. Her lower lip quivered as though she were ready to cry. "Don't kill me."

Luke almost laughed. Nine-millimeter bullets would scarcely puncture that thick hide. "Tell me where to find him," he said.

She pointed a shaking finger to the window. A single thick tear tracked down one fat cheek.

Luke rolled his eyes. He made go-ahead motions.

"Ack. Ackuh. Acapulco. Acapulco."

"Where in Acapulco?"

"Trieste Hotel."

"What's he doing there?"

"Vuh-vuh-vacation. Taking a vacation."

Luke sighed. This was not good news. "Have you ever heard of Larry Vandevere?" he asked. "Ever heard Corsica say that name?

She shook her head.

"Okay. Close your eyes now."

She began to blubber in earnest. She reached out to him, beseeching. "Please! Please!"

"If you open your eyes, or scream, or do anything at all in the next five minutes, I will kill you. If I don't do it tonight, I'll do it tomorrow. If I have to track you down all next week, I'll do it. So don't even move. Understand?"

She clenched her eyes shut, nodding. Tears shone on her cheeks. She hitched and sobbed.

Luke turned the light off and left.

He was scarcely down the steps when she began to scream like some great, bellowing animal. He ran for the front door and burst outside as someone ran around the house from the beach side, a darting shadow in the dark.

Pinpoints of flame leapt from the barrel of a submachine gun and the night exploded with noise.

Luke jumped back as bullets sparked off the concrete steps in front of his feet. He aimed the VP70Z at the running figure and fired three times. The figure stumbled and fell.

Luke ran for the fence.

Larry Vandevere was awakened in the middle of the night by a hammering pain that filled his head like thunder. He jerked his eyes open, confused and groggy, unable to remember where he was or how he had gotten there. He tried to move and felt a pitchfork of pain stab through his side.

He was lying on his stomach on a damp stone floor. Harsh white light shined from a single bulb over his head.

Heavy wooden beams ran across the ceiling. The walls were made of cement block here. There was some sort of bulky metal machine over in the corner.

A furnace.

Somebody's basement.

Larry groaned, trying to sit up. His hands were tied behind his back. One of his legs had gone to sleep and felt like some heavy, dead thing connected to his body. He squirmed around on his stomach on the gritty floor, succeeding finally in rolling over. New pain surged up his spine like a heavy bolt of lightning.

It began to come back to him then.

That guy, Manning, had brought him down here and beat the living shit out of him.

It had gone on for what seemed like hours. At least he had had the decency to take the bag off Larry's head before he pounded him senseless. That way he could see the fists, see the feet, see the two-foot length of green rubber hose whistling through the air. If Manning hadn't tied his hands, Larry would have countered with some fists and feet of his own, but it had taken all his talents just to duck and dodge.

Manning was a mean son of a bitch.

Yet the galling thing of it was, Herman Munster hadn't seemed to enjoy his work at all. He had beaten Larry mechanically, without much obvious enthusiasm. As he pounded him with the hose, he had actually stopped to emit a great yawn.

Larry remembered screaming toward the end. Not conscious screams for help, or little yelps of pain, but great, racking screams against the outrage being committed on his body. That damn hose had drawn blood every time it thumped across his back. Now his white shirt was stuck to his back with wet scabs.

He sat up, wincing, trying not to move where it hurt the

most, which was just about everywhere. His ears rang like
a distant siren. He probed his mouth with his tongue and
discovered that the insides of his cheeks had been ground
up against his teeth. One front tooth wobbled as if on
small hinges.

"Knock a few of his teeth out," the man with the
terrible allergy had said. "Use the rubber hose on him."
And Manning had complied as enthusiastically as if he had
just been asked to rake the grass or wash the Rolls-Royce.
And toward the end Larry had begun to scream. Manning
didn't give the slightest shit, just went on beating him until
he passed out. Swell guy. Both of them.

Larry drew his knees up to his chest and rocked forward
to stand up. His sleeping leg came awake and began to
tingle. He hobbled across the room and slumped against
the sheet-metal wall of the huge furnace. His eyes ached in
their sockets. Both of them were puffed out to slits.
When he breathed, stitches of pain crawled up his throat.
Manning had hit him there too. Karate-chopped him across
the Adam's apple with the side of his hand. That had been
toward the end, when Larry was screaming like a loon.
Probably he had intended to shut him up. Maybe it had
worked.

Before him was a doorway that led to another basement
room. He could see a flight of wooden steps there, leading
up into blackness. He staggered over to it and looked up.
There was another door at the top.

He went up the stairs, wobbling like a drunk. At the top
he pushed on the door with his foot. A bit of old paint
flaked off on his shoe. The door held.

He turned and twisted, trying to free his hands. It was
no use. He stared at the knob, frowning. Just how do you
open a door with no hands?

He brought one knee up and fiddled with the knob,
rattling it. He bent down and tried to take the knob in his

mouth. His loose front tooth got pushed backward, stabbing him with pain. He jerked back, setting it back into place with his tongue. Now he could taste fresh blood. He turned to the side and spit over the steps to the floor below.

The door was pulled open from the outside. A sleepy-eyed Manning regarded him.

"You ready to talk turkey with the boss?" he asked.

Larry thought about it. "What if I'm not?"

"Then we repeat the process until we get it right."

Larry lunged forward, butting Manning in the face with his head. Manning fell down with a cry of surprise. Larry jumped away from him and ran.

But Manning reached out and caught his foot, jerking him down.

He fell heavily on his side on the slick linoleum floor. At least, he realized, he knew this much about the house: The basement led up to the kitchen. Big help.

"Okay, hero," Manning said, getting to his feet. Blood was running out his nose. "Now I'm really going to show you what I can do."

He dragged him down the basement steps.

Chapter 9

Luke arrived back in Phoenix the next morning red-eyed and weary. Jake met him at the airport, not looking too chipper himself. Life on crutches seemed to be wearing him out.

"Did you talk to him?" Jake asked while they waited for Luke's suitcase.

Luke shook his head. Sky Harbor International was just beginning to wake up, the huge corridors starting to fill with travelers. The morning sun shone through the big plate-glass windows, making Luke's eyes water. He had gone two nights now with only snatches of sleep. "How's Missy?"

"She cried in the night. When I got in, Frags was trying to calm her down. We took turns telling her stories, and that seemed to cheer her up. But she wants her dad pretty bad."

"So do I," Luke said.

Jake nodded agreement. "What's the next step, then?"

"We pay a little visit to Mexico, courtesy of Calvin Steeples and his wonderful flying machines. Did he get sobered up?"

"Sleeping like a log when I left."

Luke's suitcase slid down the ramp and he picked it up. "Let's go get him motivated, then."

They drove to Superstition's Base with the tape deck blasting oldies to keep them awake. When they got there, Missy was already cooking breakfast. The cabin smelled like a pancake house when they walked inside, stepping over Calvin, who was stretched out in a sleeping bag by the door, dead to the world and still reeking like a brewery. Ben Sanchez was in the recliner by the fireplace, glumly leafing through a copy of *Motor Trend*.

"Happy faces everywhere," Luke said.

Missy offered him a smile as she shoveled a spatula heaped with pancakes onto a plate. "Did you find out where he is?"

"Not yet, honey. But we will today." He nudged Calvin with a foot. "If I can get my pilot awake, that is."

Calvin sat up and rubbed his bloodshot eyes. "Oof," he grunted. "Where the hell am I?"

"In my employ," Luke said. "I'm deducting five grand for drinking on company time."

"All in the line of duty," Calvin replied, grinning. "Ah, jeez, my head. Hey, what smells so good?"

"Three dozen pancakes," Missy said. "Come and get 'em."

They assembled at the counter and dug in. "How about Frags?" Jake asked as he poured syrup over his pancakes. "Want me to ring him?"

"No, I'll spell him in a minute," Luke said. "Soon as I get the taste of airline food out of my mouth."

"What did you find out?" Ben asked.

Luke told them what had happened during the night, omitting the gunplay for Missy's sake. "I'll bet Corsica spends a lot of time away from home," he finished, grinning. "You should have seen his wife." He spread his hands. "Large Marge."

They laughed. "So I guess you'll be going down to that hotel in Acapulco," Ben said. "What does that leave for us? Sit and wait and still collect our pay?"

"Hardly," Luke said. "Cal, when you're done, you'll need to preflight the Huey. A guy like Corsica doesn't go on vacation alone—he'll have plenty of goons watching over him. We're going to drop in on him, and I mean literally drop in. Jake can stay here and keep Missy and his bum leg company. Ben, you'll play door gunner. As for Frags, he's got enough to keep him busy for a long time."

"Door gunner?" Ben said, his voice cracking a bit. "An aerial assault on Acapulco?" He smiled, thinking about it. "Hell, I'm game."

Calvin almost choked. "Hold on, you two. As I recall, Acapulco is full of people. Tourist types. Gringos spending money. Japanese guys taking pictures. If we go shoot up one of their hotels, we could get in trouble. Like with the Mexican Air Force, if you get my drift. The Huey won't stand much of a chance against Fl6s, tough old bird or not. I say we table the motion until a competency hearing can be held."

"Always the worrier," Jake put in, and nudged him with an elbow.

Missy giggled. Luke smiled, glad to see her so cheerful this morning. It would always be the nights when the loneliness hit worst. His smile began to fade. What if Larry was dead? How would her nights be then?

"Eat up, guys," he said. "We've got things to do."

The phone rang a short while later. Luke went over to it, wiping his mouth with a napkin. "Yo."

"Tran Cao here, Luke. Remember me?"

"I think so. Are you that short little guy who's going to spend the rest of his life in a cave?"

"Not anymore. I've almost got the FBI code cracked. I've narrowed it down to two erroneous digits, though I don't know which position yet."

"How about the DMV job?"

"Patience, please. I can only work one miracle at a time."

"I expect two from all employees on a daily basis, but for now I'll let it go. Getting hungry?"

"I passed that stage yesterday afternoon. When are you going to install a vending machine down here?"

"Put that in the suggestion box," Luke said, chuckling. "I'll bring you down some pancakes, if you like."

"I do like. Heavy on the butter. And I need a carton of Marlboros, if anybody's going to the store. If I run out, I walk off the job."

"Okay, Jake can take care of that."

"One other thing, Luke."

"What's that?"

"Could he pick me up some betel nuts? I've decided to give up totally. Give up quitting, I mean. I'm too old to be taught new tricks. Besides, I'm going out of my mind down here."

"I'll see what I can do. They might have a Vietnamese specialty shop downtown."

"Okay. Out here."

Luke hung up.

"Did you change your mind yet?" Calvin asked him. "About invading Acapulco, I mean?"

Luke shook his head. "Not on your life."

Jake did Calvin the favor of pulling the vintage Huey out of the underground hangar with the electric tow vehicle, while Missy stood out in the sunlight watching it roll up the gentle slope that ended at the rim of the runway. On tiptoe, she peeked inside as Calvin stripped the tarpaulin away to uncover the copter's green skin.

"It's so *big*," she blurted.

Calvin smiled. "She's tiny compared to something really big, like a Chinook or a SkyCrane, but she gets the job done.'' His smile disappeared and he muttered under his breath: ''But not against F16s, or SAMs, or 30-mm cannons.''

It had been a SAM-7 Strela rocket that brought down the giant C5-A he had been piloting in Vietnam. That encounter with a lone surface-to-air missile had not only junked his plane into a rice paddy but cost him three years in a North Vietnamese cage as well. According to what the press had been saying lately about Mexican prisons, they weren't much better.

And he had no desire ever to go to prison again. It would be easier to face a horde of fat men from the IRS than face one sadistic guard with a fan belt or length of chain in his hands. Luke seemed to be taking this thing as a joke, that was the mysterious thing. Surely he knew the danger involved.

''What's that thing?'' Missy asked, pointing to the side of the door.

''M60 mount,'' Calvin replied. He indicated Jake, who was driving up the ramp with the 7.62-mm machine gun balanced across the front of the tow vehicle. He stopped, and Calvin hoisted it up.

''Yuck,'' Missy said. ''I hate guns.''

''Yeah, but the bad guys don't,'' Jake called out as he turned around. ''So we gotta outgun them.''

She frowned, pondering the logic of that, while Calvin hopped aboard and hooked the M60 in its mount.

''Have you ever shot anybody?'' she asked after a bit.

'' 'Fraid I have, Missy. But only because I had to.''

''Did he scream?''

''Huh?'' Calvin looked down at her. Kids always asked the darnedest questions. ''I guess I don't know, Missy. Besides, it's something you shouldn't be concerned about. Not at your age, anyway.''

She made a sour face. "My daddy won't talk about it, either. He tells me to drop it."

"Might be good advice."

"Then why do people always kill each other if they don't like to talk about it?"

Squatted in the door, Calvin scratched his head. "Tell you what," he said. "Why don't we just drop it?"

"Phooey," she said, and walked away, passing Luke and Ben, who were walking up the ramp.

"All set?" Luke asked, squinting in the morning sun. He had a revolver holstered at his waist, and a pair of binoculars slung around his neck. Ben had his familiar Chief's Special.

"Pretty quick now. Are you ready to go?"

"No time like the present."

"Where's the usual arsenal? Where's your trusty M203?"

"Today we travel light. Besides, do you want to start a war down there? We can't shoot up Acapulco in broad daylight and get away with it, you know."

"Do I." Calvin breathed a sigh of relief. "I take it you haven't gone insane after all." He patted the M60. "What's this for, then? Just for show?"

"Hopefully. If there's anything the Mafia respects, it's got to be a machine gun. I doubt if we'll even have to use it."

Jake drove up and loaded five ammo boxes into the Huey, grunting as he gave them a shove across the floor.

"But then again, you never know," Luke said, giving Calvin a wink.

At roughly the same moment that Luke, Ben, and Calvin were lifting off from Superstitions Base for their eight-hour flight to Acapulco, Mel Corsica, their target, was having one of his attacks.

These attacks took the form of intense rage. A fat man

with drooping sallow skin and receding gray hair, Corsica would turn fiery red, his brown eyes would become shot through with bright snaps of scarlet, his lips and eyelids would take on a pale shade of blue, and he would scream while spit flew from his lips. The older he got, the more often these attacks came over him. At sixty-four, he was having them quite often now.

"*Fuck*!" he was currently screaming. He was in Suite 117 of the Trieste Hotel in Acapulco, a structure whose tall, pyramidal shape hinted at an influence of Mayan architecture. The hotel was one of a chain of hotels that lined the curving beach, which was busy with tourists in colorful swimsuits. The beach was dotted with what looked like unfinished tepees, palm-frond roofs on stilts, under which tourists sat safe from the glaring sun in wooden deck chairs. At this time some of them were craning around in their chairs, peeking over their sunglasses at the Trieste Hotel, from which the sound of screaming was emanating. It sounded like someone was being killed.

"*Fucking Goddamn son of a bitch*!" Corsica shrieked, rattling the walls of his hotel suite. He was wearing a large bath towel over his ponderous belly. Below it, his skinny legs stuck out, as white as a fish's belly. The towel had come untucked and he was holding it up with both hands while he stalked around his hotel room kicking things. Two of his lieutenants, wearing dark suits, looked on helplessly.

"*Oh, you cocksucker*!" Mel Corsica bellowed. He kicked a nightstand and it fell over, taking the blue Trieste telephone, which had caused all this trouble, crashing down with it. He grabbed his foot with both hands and hopped. His towel slithered to the floor. His lieutenants looked away discreetly.

"*Ow! Ow! Ow! Fuck! Tony*!"

Tony, one of the lieutenants, squared his padded shoulders. "Yes, Mr. Corsica?"

"My underpants, goddammit. Find me my underpants."

"Yes, Mr. Corsica." Tony went to a dresser and began scouting through drawers.

"Harry!"

Harry straightened.

"Why do things always have to come fucking unglued while I'm away? Do you know who that was on the phone? Know who it was that got me out of the shower?"

"It sounded like you were talking to your wife, Mr. Corsica."

"Yeah! Yeah! Chaos! Fuck!"

Tony handed him a pair of voluminous boxer shorts. Dancing from foot to foot, Corsica managed to get them on. "They've had her on tranquilizers since last night. Somebody broke in, threatened to kill her. Mike's dead, and Lenny's got two bullets in him. Some guy all painted black, she said. Looked like a cat burglar, she said. Scared the living shit out of her, she said. She wants me to come home."

He raised his hands beseechingly toward the ceiling. "Why me, God? I get one, maybe two vacations a year, and a cat burglar comes along to fuck me up. Is there no justice, God? Is there?"

"Your pants, Mr. Corsica," Tony said, and handed him a pair of dark trousers.

Corsica eyed them hatefully. "Oh, no. I came down here for nothing but two weeks of Bermuda shorts, and that's what I'm going to wear. Harry!"

"Still here, Mr. Corsica."

"You and Tony, you catch a plane today. You fly back and see what's been going on. You find out who this cat burglar guy is. If he's from one of the other families, we've got a war on our hands. I pray he's not from a family. I pray he's just a guy looking to heist the family jewels. Either way, I want him. Nobody breaks in on Mel Corsica and walks away. Nobody."

"Right, Mr. Corsica."

"If it's family business, we'll handle it in a family way. If it's a burglar, call the cops. It's their damn fault, anyway. There's too much crime in Chicago. When somebody takes a chunk out of Mel Corsica's ass, there's too much crime."

"Right, Mr. Corsica."

"Well? Going to stand there all day? Move your asses!"

They hustled out. Grumbling, Corsica dressed himself in crazy-colored Bermuda shorts, a Hawaiian shirt, knee socks, and his customary black Oxfords. Still grumbling, he plopped a straw hat on his head.

"Fine fucking vacation," he growled at himself in the mirror by the door.

He went out to try to enjoy himself on the beach.

After a refueling stop in Torreon, and another in Morelia, Deadly Force Incorporated was on the last leg of the nine-hundred-mile journey to find Mel Corsica. Helicopter flight, exhilarating at first, soon becomes tedious, a fact Luke had discovered quickly in Vietnam. Despite the wind blasting through the side windows, the hot Mexican sun kept the cockpit too warm for comfort, and although the combination of the howling gas turbine and the flapping rotors made enough noise to wake the dead, it was easy to drowse.

Luke reached over and knocked on Calvin's flight helmet. "Still awake?"

Through the headset Calvin's voice sounded tired. "Now I know why they won't let you drink twenty-four hours before a flight. I feel like I've got the flu."

"You'll survive. Ben?"

"Ready in the rear."

"Okay, I see the coastline."

The broad panorama of the Pacific unveiled itself before them, a curving band of dark blue on the horizon.

"Just follow the coast now," Luke said to Calvin.

"What kind of altitude?"

"Hundred feet or so. I need to see faces."

Calvin glanced at him. "You've met the dude before?"

"I've seen his picture."

"Oh, I just love this. You realize we're going to get a lot of people pissed, don't you?"

Luke shrugged. "Has that ever stopped us before?"

"Guess not." He eased the Huey left, dropping down toward the rocky coast. "There it is, up ahead," he said. "And it does look crowded."

"Okay, slow her down." Luke put his binoculars to his eyes. "Stay over the water to keep the sand from blowing too bad. Dig?"

"Yeah, I dig."

Calvin manuevered the craft slowly down the water line. Behind a jutting volcanic bluff, the long semicircle of Acapulco Beach began, its white-brown sand a shining ribbon under the afternoon sun. A row of majestic hotels bulked up behind the beach. The city itself glittered on the western side, nestled against the mountains of the Sierra Madre del Sur. Luke nodded appreciatively. It was a beautiful sight. For Corsica, no doubt a welcome change from Chicago's drabness.

"Shit," Luke muttered.

"What's wrong?"

"Most of them are old men with gray hair."

"I can see that. Man, look at the babes those rich old dudes got. Is this a topless beach?"

"Anything goes in Acapulco."

"Holy cow," Ben murmured in the back, leaning out the side door.

They drifted over the turquoise water, the wind from the rotor beating it into frothy ripples and creating a minor sandstorm on the beach itself. Sunbathers sat up in surprise, their blankets flapping. A red beach umbrella tipped over and skittered away. Beach furniture folded in on itself. People pointed and stared.

"I don't like this," Calvin muttered. His eyes bulged as he spotted a nude woman trying to wrap herself in a towel. He jerked the collective pitch stick up, creating more wind. Her flapping towel blew out of her hands. He grinned. "But then again, maybe I do."

"Not so bumpy, dammit."

"Party pooper."

"Wait, there's a likely suspect." Luke pointed. "Get me closer."

Calvin rolled his eyes. "People are gonna shit, Luke."

"Screw 'em."

The Huey drifted low over the beach. A tornado of sand erupted beneath it. Umbrellas, beach balls, towels, blankets, and deck chairs scattered crazily in the wind. A row of sun shelters lost their thatched roofs and collapsed in a heap of stilts. People scurried away, blinded by sand, thumping into each other, falling down. The noise of women screaming penetrated the turbine's roar.

"Could be him," Luke said. He pointed to the ground. "Set us down."

Calvin settled the Huey lightly on the beach. Luke unplugged the intercom cord from his helmet, swung his door open, and hopped out. He ran across the neatly swept sand to a fat, gray-haired man who was stumbling around rubbing his eyes. Calvin saw them exchange words.

Luke unholstered his pistol and jammed it in the fat man's stomach. The fat man fell to his knees with his hands clasped together, beseeching. Luke ran back to the chopper, holstering his revolver.

He climbed back in. "Not him," he said after he had plugged his helmet in. "Too chicken."

Calvin lifted the Huey into the air again and let it drift

sideways, back over the water. Now he could see someone running their way, a man in a tan uniform with a black Sam Browne belt crossed over his shoulder. A holster flapped at his side.

"Local constable," Luke said. "Let's move."

"Gladly. Where to?"

"Down the beach. If Corsica's not here, we'll try his hotel."

"What about the cop?"

"Ben can take care of him."

Calvin stared at Luke, feeling his heart sink. First they destroy the beach, then they gun down a cop with a machine gun, then they leisurely stop off at a hotel and get caught. By his estimation, they would be in prison for one thousand years, give or take.

The cop unholstered his pistol as he ran. He aimed at the sky. Smoke puffed out the barrel.

"Warning shot," Luke said. "Ben?"

"Yes, boss?"

"Give him one of your own."

"Will do."

Calvin heard the M60 thunder. Sand jumped up at the Mexican cop's feet. He tripped over his own shoes and went sprawling, then got up and ran away.

"Okay," Luke said. He lifted his binoculars. "Down the beach."

Groaning, Calvin eased the copter along the beachfront, scattering people and objects. Luke studied everything calmly through the binoculars.

"There he is," he said at last. "White socks and black shoes. The guy with a straw hat on his head."

"Down?" Calvin asked glumly.

"Down."

A fresh circle of beach was swept clean by the rotor wash as they landed. People scurried madly away. The man Luke had in mind was backing away, holding one fat arm across his face to shield it. In his free hand he held a tall glass with a slice of pineapple on the rim. It was sloshing all over his hand. Calvin knew this couldn't be the right guy. He was dressed like a tourist from Arkansas.

Luke got out and ran to him. The man executed a shuffling turn and tried to run. Luke drew his revolver and pressed it to the man's back. He stopped, turning slowly around. He raised his hands. His hat blew off his head. Luke shouted something to a couple of bodyguards types, who backed off quickly.

They walked to the copter. Calvin looked back into the cabin as Luke pushed the man inside, spilling his drink across the floor. The fat guy looked like he was about to have a heart attack.

"Take her up," Luke shouted, pointing up with a thumb.

Calvin jerked the Huey into the sky.

Mel Corsica was indeed having an attack, but it had nothing to do with his heart.

He had seen the army-green helicopter as it rounded the bluffs at the northern rim of the beach but had dismissed it as some kind of Mexican Army craft working the port, maybe for drug smugglers or the like. Corsica's own drug-smuggling operations were conducted on land, so he had no interest in what occurred on the sea. If some poor bastard was about to have his operation split wide open by the Mexican feds, it was his own problem.

But then that cop had gone charging past. From the shade of his sun shelter, Corsica had watched this with growing interest. The cop had shot into the air. The helicopter had answered with a burst of machine-gun fire.

A *revolucion*? A Mexican coup with Mel Corsica stuck in the middle? Please God, no.

Then the helicopter landed not twenty feet away. A guy

dressed in jeans and a red T-shirt and wearing a green helmet ran over. And now, this helmeted weirdo had pushed him inside the helicopter, where some kind of grinning Indian manned the machine gun, and made him spill his drink. And the goddamn drinks in Acapulco didn't come cheap.

"Get your fucking paws off me!" Corsica shouted at him, lying on his back on the warm metal floor. This helicopter was a noisy son of a bitch. You had to scream just to get yourself heard. "Leave me the hell alone!"

"Shut up," the guy said, and hollered at the pilot to take them up.

Corsica's stomach bottomed out against his spine. It was like jumping on a Ferris wheel going a bit too fast. He swallowed. It suddenly came to him that he had to piss, and badly.

The guy took his helmet off. "Where's Larry Vandevere?"

"Who the fuck?" Corsica shouted back.

The guy jerked him up and set him on his knees. Strong son of a bitch, Corsica had to admit. Mel Corsica was not an easy man to jerk around.

"Larry Vandevere, I said."

"Who wants to know?"

The guy grabbed the back of Corsica's neck and forced his head out the open door. He almost threw up. The beauty of Acapulco's beach was a receding aerial postcard below. The helicopter was barreling straight up, as fast as it would go.

"Talk, or out you go."

"Okay, okay!"

He got pulled back in. His bladder thumped like an overstretched balloon. "Who did you say?"

"Larry Vandevere."

"Never heard of him."

Out the door again. Corsica squeezed his eyes shut. "Help!"

In again. Corsica's head swam. He took a faltering breath. "Tell me who this guy is, and maybe I'll remember."

"He's a Chicago cop. He works the South Side. The cops are being paid off, and he's disappeared. I think you're the asshole who disappeared him."

"Not me! I swear!"

"Why are you buying the cops? What do you want on the South Side?"

Corsica shook his head. "You've got the wrong guy. The South Side isn't shit. I mean, we sell some dope down there, maybe run a few hookers. But there isn't any money in the South Side. They're all too poor."

"Liar."

Corsica got shoved out again. His knees slid across the smooth metal and rested on the drop-off. He pinwheeled his arms, screaming. The rotor was a flashing blur overhead. Warm urine sprayed down one beefy leg, darkening his Bermuda shorts. The Indian laughed.

Corsica began to cry. The strong hand on his neck pulled him back inside. "Talk, dammit!"

He racked his brains for something to say that would end this horror. "There's only one guy I know of who's got an interest in the South Side. He's a big, rich son of a bitch, one of those multimillionaires. A real-estate developer. Some kind of political nut too. He buys off the cops when he needs to. Maybe he's who you're after."

The two men exchanged glances. Corsica saw the Indian shrug.

"What's his name?" the one with the hand asked.

"Shelmont, I think. Jonathan Shelmont. I swear he's your guy.

The cool barrel of a revolver was pressed hard into

Corsica's throat. He swallowed, cringing. What a way to end a glorious and successful life.

The strong man pressed his lips to Corsica's ear. "If you're lying, I'll hunt you down again and kill you. Understand?"

Corsica nodded meekly.

"Take her down!" the guy shouted.

The helicopter fell from the sky. Corsica covered his face with his hands and screamed. Thirty seconds later he was pushed out. He screamed and screamed until he thought his throat would burst. Urine trailed him as he fell.

He performed the world's biggest belly flop thirty yards from the beach. A thousand onlookers gasped, then cheered when he bobbed to the surface and began to swim.

As he struggled up the beach, and just before he collapsed facedown in the warm, wet sand, he had one final coherent thought: to get those bastards if it was the last thing he ever did.

Chapter 10

It was nearly midnight when the chopper touched down again at Superstitions Base. As the turbine wound down, Luke dragged his helmet wearily off his head and set it on the floor beside his seat. Calvin clicked the instrument lights off and yawned.

"Have we earned any shut-eye?" he asked.

"You two have, yeah." Luke looked over to the cabin. Lights were burning in the windows. "Looks like Jake waited up for us. I'm going to go down below and see what Tran's come up with."

"Want me to drag this thing back in the hangar?"

Luke shook his head. "Let it wait until morning. Everybody's dead on their feet."

"That's for sure." He clambered out, groaning, and joined Ben. Together they walked to the cabin.

Luke got out, feeling stiff and old. He wondered if it hadn't been a monumental waste of time, this trip to the Mexican coast to talk to an old fat man. He felt sure Corsica didn't have Larry; the aging Mafia chief had been scared to death and would have talked if he'd had anything to say. And the lead on this other guy, this Jonathan Shelmont—it might very well be a dead end. What would a multimillionaire want with a Chicago cop? In his fright Corsica probably tossed out the first name that came to his mind.

Luke ran his hands over his bristly hair as he walked across the airstrip, trying to brush the cobwebs out of his brain. Three days work now, and still no positive leads. Larry could be in Timbuktu by now. Perhaps this detective work was best left to the detectives.

He came to the steel door that opened on the tunnel to the command center, and was punching in the code when the bolts were thrown back with a clank and the door swung inward. Tran Cao stood there, looking decidedly stooped and shrunken. He fastened bleary eyes on Luke. An unlit Marlboro hung from his mouth. The smell of stale smoke drifted out of the tunnel behind him.

"You keep any lighter fluid around?" he asked. He produced his Marine Corps Zippo and sparked it a few times. "Mine's deader than shit."

Luke shrugged. "Jake smokes those big stogies of his, so he might have some. Any luck with the FBI?"

"You kidding? Two numbers out of sync, and I still don't know which ones. The Cray's going to blow a fuse at this rate."

"How long do you estimate it'll take?"

Tran rubbed his chin. "Hard to say. We got lucky once, but it looks like our luck's not holding. Two wrong numbers in a series of ten leaves a lot of room for guesswork. But we can do it, I think. We just need more time." He pressed his fist to his mouth suddenly and doubled over as a fit of coughing overcame him. "Damn," he said when it had passed. "These things are going to kill me." He took the cigarette out of his mouth and crushed it in his hand.

Luke smiled. "Did Jake get you that carton?"

"Yeah, I've got plenty. But don't ever think Phoenix has betel nuts. I'd kill for a mouthful of that."

"Sorry." He patted Tran's shoulder consolingly. "Go take a nap, okay? I'll baby-sit the Cray for a few hours. You can dream about betel nuts."

"Sounds good." Tran passed him, then turned. "Oh, I got through to the Illinois Department of Motor Vehicles, but I don't think it will do you any good."

Luke's heart jumped. "What did you find out?"

"That plate belongs to some outfit called Associated Industries. Rental car, like you said."

Luke frowned. "Doesn't sound like a rental agency to me."

"It's not Avis or Hertz, that's for sure. Probably some local outfit."

"Did you pull an address?"

"It's laying on the printer. Someplace in Chicago. West Jackson Boulevard, I think."

"That's downtown." Luke slapped a fist into his palm. "Tran, that's not a car rental agency. It's a company. A big company in Chicago."

"So?"

"This might be the break we've been working for. Did the Department of Motor Vehicles give any names? Chief executive officer of the company or anything?"

Tran spread his hands. "I got everything they had, and the only name was Associated Industries. Who are you looking for?"

"A guy named Jonathan Shelmont." Luke's eyes narrowed as he thought of something. "Hey, Tran, have you still got a line open to the DMV?"

"No, but I've got the entry code, so I can reestablish whenever you want."

"Then come on and do it."

Tran groaned but followed him down. In the command

center he seated himself at the Cray's CRT screen and poised his hands over the keyboard. "Okay, tell me what you want."

"Open a line first. Then get a list of all the vehicles registered to Jonathan Shelmont."

Tran typed the entry code, waited while it cleared, then filed the request. Within seconds the screen began to fill with information.

Tran squinted at it. "Here's one dude who owns a lot of cars. Mercedes, a lot of them. Wait, here's a Rolls. What's a Lynxburgh-Ducat Excalibur?"

"Damned if I know. Anything show co-ownership?"

"Let's see. Shelmont . . . Shelmont . . . Shelmont . . . Shelmont and Associated Industries, Limited . . . Shelmont—"

Luke slapped him on the back. Tran swiveled in his chair, smiling uncertainly. "Is that what you were looking for?"

"Exactly what I was looking for. Jonathan Shelmont and Associated Industries are one and the same, and Corsica wasn't lying. Now we know *who's* got Missy's dad. And we've got a pretty good idea *why*. So there's only one thing missing."

"Yeah? What's that?"

"*Where*, Tran. We don't know where."

Tran dug a cigarette out of his shirt pocket and stuck it in his mouth. "So how we going to find out?"

Luke patted the Cray's steel console. "By getting that FBI feed, Tran. Corsica said this Shelmont guy was into weird politics. Rich or not, he's likely to be in the FBI files. This is exactly the kind of shit they keep tabs on." He grinned. "We're almost there, buddy. We've just got to keep plugging."

Tran sighed. He pulled his lighter out and thumbed it a few times. "Shit! When am I going to get that fluid?"

Luke gave him an evil smile. "You get your lighter fluid," he said, "as soon as I get that feed. Deal?"

Tran refused to shake on it.

The break came at quarter to four in the morning.

Luke was drowsing at the keyboard, watching the screen flash its endless error message as the nearly correct code was constantly resubmitted, thinking idly that a bell should be rigged up in the cabin to end this useless waiting. Tran had taken a chair to Luke's right and was softly snoring with his chin on his chest. The Cray whirred gently as it worked. The cavern seemed dark and full of shadows this late at night, but Luke knew it was an illusion: Even on the brightest afternoons no daylight ever penetrated this deep.

The message on the screen changed without fanfare: ACCESS GRANTED.

Luke stared at it, blinking sleepily, not yet comprehending what had happened. He sat up straighter, rubbing the stubble of whiskers on his cheeks with both hands.

"Tran?"

Tran slept on.

"Wake up, man. We've done it."

Tran shifted in his chair, mumbling Vietnamese words. Luke poked his shoulder. "Hey, Frags! Frags!"

"What?"

"Time for that victory cigarette. The FBI mainframe is ours."

"Yeah?" Tran sat up. His eyes were as red as spring tomatoes. "No shit?"

"No shit at all. Here, park yourself."

Luke got up and let Tran seat himself at the keyboard. "Open a memory channel," he told him. "Tired as we are, we're bound to forget half of this."

Tran typed a command. "Okay, memory channel waiting."

"Ask what it knows about Jonathan Shelmont."

Tran's fingers darted over the keyboard. The Cray beeped in response. The screen filled, casting dim white light over his face. At the bottom right of the screen the word MORE pulsed off and on like a small beacon.

"He's on file, all right," Tran said. "Plenty."

"Run it through quick," Luke said. "Let's see what we're facing."

Tran typed a command. The screen blurred into new lines, faded, blurred again. New data flashed on, disappeared, then flashed on again. The screen blinked like a strobe light.

"Christ," Luke muttered. "This guy's an encyclopedia."

Tran looked up at him. "Want me to dump it into memory?"

"Yeah, dump the whole mess, then print it. This will take some study."

Tran pressed a key. On the computer bank to Luke's right, lights winked on and the Cray's huge spools of memory tape began to jerk clockwise. The faint plastic smell of warming electrical circuits drifted up in the air, pulled by the ventilators. The screen hesitated while the tapes caught up, then strobed again.

"Got it," Tran said half a minute later. "The channel's empty."

Luke nodded. "Okay, now run one on Associated Industries."

Tran bent over the keyboard. "Here it comes."

The screen flashed briefly.

"That's it?"

"What does the FBI care about a car-rental agency?"

"Asshole." Grinning, Luke went over to the printer table and adjusted the paper. A thought struck him and he straightened. "Hey, Tran, can you cross-ref everything?"

"Huh?"

"Have the Cray screen all existing FBI files for the name Jonathan Shelmont. Then have it screen everything for Associated Industries. That way we'd have the whole poop."

"Whole poop?"

"You know. Everything pertinent."

"That I understand." He took a deep breath, seemed to consider, then exhaled. "Could be done, I guess."

"How quick?"

The Vietnamese turned, typed briefly, then turned again. "About that quick, I guess."

The screen began to flash madly, creating a stuttering light show in the darkened command center. The tape spools whirled. Luke turned his bloodshot eyes away from the screen until it was done.

"Got it?"

"Every byte. Anything else?"

"That ought to do it. Unless you have suggestions."

Tran stood up. "I suggest sleep."

Luke nodded. "You've earned it. Give me a printer feed, and you can hit the sack."

Tran turned back, shuffling like an old man, and typed a command. Beside Luke, the printer jumped to life, its dot-matrix head buzzing back and forth across the paper with a noise that, for Luke, would forever remind him of the man-eating mosquitoes of Vietnam. He offered the doctor a congratulatory smile. "You're number one, Frags."

Tran nodded sleepily and plodded away. "You bet, Luke. Number one."

Even at two hundred and thirty characters per second, it took the big NEC printer two hours to print everything out. Luke read it all, woozy with fatigue, passing the big fanfold sheets from hand to hand to pile at his feet.

Jonathan Shelmont's life lay exposed before him. The

FBI had done a good job. The man was a radical and a malcontent. Worse than that, he was rich enough to do something about it. Guys like this, they could be dangerous. Give a man enough weird ideas and enough money, and just sit back and watch what he can do.

Luke raised his head with a hint of a smile touching the corners of his mouth.

Plenty of people in the world would say Luke Simpson fell into the same category. Rich, perhaps a bit eccentric, perhaps a bit malcontented, perhaps a bit . . . dangerous.

Perhaps a lot dangerous.

Hundreds of dead men would testify to that, if they could.

His eyes darted over to the computer keyboard. He got up, letting the paper fall in a heap on the floor, and sauntered to it. He stared at the message on the screen, which said simply that it was waiting. Waiting for input.

He typed in his own name. He realized that it was ridiculous, that he should be putting together a plan of action to save Larry, that there was no time left to waste, that maybe too much time already had been wasted. Missy was up above, waiting, trusting. The whole Deadly Force team was under contract, on the payroll, biding their time. The CIA had their finger in the pie too. No, there was no time here for nonsense, no time for useless snooping.

He sighed. He scratched behind one ear.

After some deliberation he pressed the input key.

The computer whirred. Lights flashed on the console.

The screen went dead.

Then, after a moment, it lighted up again: FILE REQUIRES NS-12 CLEARANCE. INPUT CLEARANCE CODE FOR DELIVERY.

He smiled grimly. They had him, all right. But only the top people of the government were allowed to see who he was. In this category you might find the director of the

CIA, the director of the FBI, the director of the NSA. In this category you might find the President himself. And the Vice President, too, and a few select members of congress on special intelligence committees.

Bigwigs, all of them. Hot turds in that steaming pile of shit called Washington.

And now Luke was one of them.

He went back to his chair and his pile of paper with a sour taste building in his mouth. His smile hung on, mostly teeth now. In his drive to get away from the bureaucratic bullshit, he had managed to dig himself even deeper.

In the computer's mind, at least, he was one of *them*.

The communications console beside the Cray flashed a red light as he sat down. Phone call, ringing up in the cabin as well, where everyone was sleeping. He went over to it before it could wake anyone up and punched a button.

"DFI. Simpson here."

"Mr. Simpson?" The voice rang hollowly through the speaker mounted in the console. "Devlin here."

"Who?"

"Devlin. We met three days ago at your facility. I helicoptered in, as you recall."

Luke nodded tiredly. "The CIA guy. What now?"

"I need a progress report."

Luke massaged his forehead with his fingertips, biting back several nasty words that came to mind. "Do you always call in the middle of the night?"

"It's seven o'clock in Washington, Mr. Simpson. The report, please."

"What would you like to hear?"

Devlin hesitated. "Are the Director's fears justified? Do we have Russian involvement in the crime wave?"

"You've got to be kidding," Luke said.

"I take it that means no."

"You can take it any way you like."

"May I tell the Director how you arrived at this conclusion?"

Luke rubbed his eyes and yawned. "I found it in a fortune cookie."

Devlin cleared his throat. "I'm trying to appreciate your humor, Mr. Simpson, but to be frank with you, I don't like it. We're discussing highly sensitive national security matters here. You were hired to fulfill a specific mission, and I feel I'm justified in asking for a report on your progress to date."

"Perhaps you are. But I make it a policy not to tell anyone what I'm doing until I'm done. You'll get your report when I decide to give it to you."

"And when might that be?" Devlin asked brusquely.

"When I'm damn good and ready."

There was a long silence. Then: "How about our missing operative?"

Luke shrugged to himself. How about the missing operative? So far they'd turned up nothing on him. But to be honest, they hadn't really been looking. Yet if this Jonathan Shelmont was bold enough to kidnap a Chicago cop, why shouldn't he be bold enough to kidnap a CIA man? Find one and you just might find the other. "I have several leads," Luke said.

"Be specific, please."

"No."

"Really, Mr. Simpson, there's no reason I should have to put up with this. I—"

"You're right," Luke interrupted.

He severed the connection.

By eleven o'clock the members of DFI had assembled in the small underground amphitheater that served as Deadly Force's briefing room. The south wall was occupied by a large silver screen. Two rows of plush theater chairs lined the opposite wall. Overhead, a projector trailing a thick cable hung from a steel boom, ready to light the screen with information fed to it from the Cray. Once again Tran Cao was manning the huge computer in the adjoining command center. An open intercom connected the two areas.

"Hear me all right, Frags?" Luke said. He was standing to the side of the screen with a small pencil laser in his hand. He aimed it at the screen and clicked it on and off, satisfied to see a dot of intense red light appear.

"Loud and clear," Tran replied.

"Jake, dim the light, will you?"

Grumbling, Jake got out of his chair. Missy was seated beside him, looking at everything with wide eyes. Before Jake could assemble his crutches and hobble to the switch on the wall Calvin went over to it and turned the knob. The overhead bulbs dimmed to a pale orange.

"Sorry," Luke said in the sudden darkness. "I keep forgetting."

Jake sat back down. "And they say *I'm* getting old."

Ben chuckled, sitting off to Luke's left with one snake-skin boot crossed atop the other over the back of a chair. "When's the last time you got some sleep, Luke?"

Luke snorted. "Don't ask." He clicked his laser pencil on and trained it at the bottom of the screen. "Everybody set?"

They nodded.

"Start the show, Tran."

The screen filled with light. Small black dots began to appear on it, beamed there by the Cray, multiplying themselves into a grainy picture, like a bad newspaper photograph. "Here we have the extraordinarily rich Jonathan Shelmont," Luke said when it was done. "File photo courtesy of the FBI, thank you very much. His age in this photo is twenty-six years."

"No wonder it looks so bad," Calvin said. "How old's the rich bastard now?"

"Twenty-nine," Luke said, and saw Jake sneer.

"Daddy's money. One of those lucky brats."

"Hardly. Shelmont didn't have a pot to piss in ten years ago. The man is a self-made millionaire. Billionaire, probably, if you include his secret Swiss accounts. He made his fortune, as many do, in real estate. In 1978, he purchased a two-bedroom rental house in Barrington, Illinois, his first real-estate transaction. By 1980, he owned sixteen homes and was able to quit his job as a print-shop apprentice to become a full-time landlord. Eighteen months later he bought his first condominium."

Calvin frowned. "How? You're talking a lot of money."

"I know," Luke agreed. "Shelmont is a ruthless bargainer, a genius when it comes to real estate. He arranged financing through six separate banks, using his rental properties as security. The deal was closed before the banks realized they were all holding the same collateral. Rather than call Shelmont on the carpet and face a massive default, they let the situation ride. Meanwhile Shelmont purchased an office complex on West Jackson Boulevard in Chicago using his condo as security. All this was done so fast, the banks didn't have time to coordinate with each other. By the time the true facts came out, they were carrying million-dollar mortgages and didn't dare rock the boat for fear of default."

"Isn't that rather illegal?" Jake asked.

"Damn right it is. And if Shelmont had been your ordinary shyster, the whole tightwire would have collapsed overnight. Happens all the time. But Shelmont made good on his loans, so that by 1984, he was purchasing properties worth millions the way most people buy eggs—by the dozen. Next screen, Tran."

The screen went white, then was intersected by a growing network of lines. The finished product, completed in seconds, was a map.

"Lake Michigan shorefront," Luke said. "Every foot here is roughly a mile." He aimed his laser pencil at a crudely triangular outline several feet from the mainland. "As seen from above, this is Guiles Island, two miles off the North Chicago shore. Three years ago Shelmont bought the island from the gravel company who owned it. It was a moonscape of old gravel pits and rusting machinery. He spent a fortune to turn it into a private Eden. It's here where he and his army are headquartered."

"Army?" Calvin blurted. "The dude's got his own *army*?"

Luke chuckled. "That's what Shelmont thinks it is. As far as the FBI can estimate, he's hired fifteen to twenty goons to walk around toting SMGs. They wear some kind of uniform, very unmilitary. An undercover bureau man went there posing as a bank official and reported back that Shelmont's people look like an army of pizza-delivery boys. They wear red pants."

"Red pants?" Calvin laughed. "That wouldn't have done them much good in 'Nam, huh?"

"To each his own, I guess. Somehow the colors all tie in with Shelmont's politics. He's somewhat of a radical. Flip it, Tran."

This time the screen etched out lines of print. "This is a facsimile of a leaflet Shelmont had printed up and mailed last year. His mailing list consisted exclusively of rich and influential men in the Chicago area. The gist of it was this: It was Shelmont's invitation to join his crackpot movement, the Achievers of the New Order."

"I get it," Jake said. "Another blankety-blank Nazi."

"Missy's presence has tamed you remarkably, Jake. But no, you're not right at all. Chicago's black mayor received a leaflet. Prominent Jewish businessmen did too. Shelmont is not a Nazi, and he's not a racist. He believes in the genetic superiority of overachievers like himself. The thing has racial overtones not based on color. He believes there are two classes of people: the nonachievers and the achievers. It is his aim to force the nonachievers into a kind of exile by replacing their homes with condominiums.''

"Now I really get it," Jake growled. "Shelmont's a *nut*."

"Probably right. Like a lot of overachievers, he's mentally in outer space. Remember Howard Hughes and his phobia about germs?''

"I do," Missy said shyly. "He let his fingernails grow real long." She indicated twelve inches. "They looked like corkscrews.''

Luke nodded. "When the average guy goes nuts, they put him in a sanitarium. Rich guys don't get that lucky. They surround themselves with people who agree with them. Their insanity gets worse, but no one dares to do anything about it for fear of losing a paycheck. The same thing's happening to Shelmont.''

"Do you mean," Jake asked, "that all those Chicago bigwigs went along with him?''

"Of course not. Shelmont reserved a hotel banquet room for the first meeting of the Achievers, and nobody showed up except a few reporters and a drunk looking for the bathroom. That threw him into a tailspin. He went back to Guiles Island and brooded for a few months. Then he started buying tenement homes in the slums under the name Associated Industries.''

"That's a hell of a switch," Jake said. "From condos to slums.''

"Sure is. He's bought up whole blocks at a time. For some reason he always gets what he goes after. Nobody knows why, for sure. It looks like he intends to buy up all of south Chicago and turn it into condos and offices.''

"What about the people?" Ben asked, sitting up. "What happens to them?"

"I don't know," Luke replied. "But here's my guess, based on what you guys uncovered. Shelmont's goons terrorize the tenants into moving out. He pays the cops to look the other way. Some cops even participate, paying local hoods to speed up the process. The landlords are forced to sell to Shelmont because their renters have all left. Down go the slums, up go the condos. And Shelmont's underachievers can all go to hell, as far as he cares. Thousands of people wind up homeless and he doesn't give the slightest shit. Whoops, sorry, Missy."

She smiled. "Is that who has my daddy, Luke? That bad man?"

Luke nodded. "It sure is."

"Is he on that island, that Gilligan's Island?"

He stifled a smile. "We don't know that for sure. We won't know until we get there."

She settled back, seeming satisfied.

"Is that the deal, then?" Calvin asked. "We take the island? Just like D Day?"

"After all this time, that's finally the deal," Luke said. "We take the island, just like D Day."

He took a breath, studying faces.

"And D Day is tonight."

Chapter 11

Jonathan Shelmont stared out the window of his third-story office, nervously nibbling his lower lip.

A hazy evening sun shone over the green expanse of Guiles Island, casting long shadows. Orange light sparkled on the blue-gray water beyond the stark white rocks of the shoreline. Shelmont could remember when this island was no more than a misshapen lump of gravel, dotted with stagnant lagoons, thick with mosquitoes and wildflowers. The mosquitoes and wildflowers were gone now, and the gravel was buried beneath forty tons of sod hauled from the mainland at great expense. It had been a huge and expensive project, turning this triangular stretch of land two miles off the Chicago coast into paradise, but like all things Jonathan Shelmont attempted, it had been success-ful. He was an achiever, and achievers never failed.

He would not fail now. Not because of one stubborn cop. This thing with Vandevere had to come to an end pretty soon. It was getting scary, and Jonathan Shelmont was not a man who scared easily. It looked like they were going to have to kill him to get him out of the way.

His employee, Manning, had spent the night and most of the day torturing Larry Vandevere. He reported in regularly to say that nothing had changed, that Vandevere was still fighting back. Yet the man had to have a breaking point; all men did. For Vandevere that point might only be reached at the moment of his death. And then Jonathan Shelmont would be guilty of a federal offense.

In his career he had often bent the law. His empire had been founded on minor illegalities and petty crime. Since the Achievers of the New Order had gone swirling down the tubes, he had resorted more and more to crime in order to achieve his goals. At this very moment his men might be in the process of killing someone in Chicago. Shelmont did not keep track but felt he could safely assume several dozen peasants had already been murdered in this latest project.

Chewing his lower lip, he wondered briefly how it had come to this. His only intention had been to create a better world, one free of crime and poverty and ugliness, one populated only by achievers. For this he had been ignored, sneered at, laughed at. The press had had a hearty chuckle when the first meeting of the ANO bombed. Alone in the huge banquet hall, looking foolish and awkward in his tuxedo, racked by attacks of sneezing, Shelmont had tried to explain to the peasants of the press what kind of new order he envisioned. The next morning, every op-ed page of every Chicago paper carried jeering editorials. One, the *Sun-Times,* even had a crude cartoon of a very Hitlerian-looking Shelmont holding a globe in one hand and a whisk broom in the other. "Gonna clean up the world," the caption beneath read. Har-har, and hardy-har-har. Everybody got a good laugh at Jonathan Shelmont's expense.

No one was laughing now. No one was even looking now. Like many failed political movements, the ANO and its sole member had now gone underground.

Staring out the window, Shelmont smiled bitterly to himself. His uniformed cadre patrolled the island below on foot and in golf carts, ready to give their lives for him and his paychecks.

Peasants, all of them. Morons and thugs, the most useful type of peasant. They made him ill, but they served a purpose. When the new order had been created, he would have them killed.

He passed a hand suddenly over his eyes. What was he thinking? You cannot simply have people killed because they no longer serve a purpose. What was this recent obsession with killing, with death? There were nights when Jonathan Shelmont woke up out of a nightmare with a scream building behind his lips, his eyes wide and staring in the dark. Soaked with cold sweat, he would writhe beneath the covers as hideous mental images sprouted in his mind with awful clarity. He would see himself uncovered, exposed to the world as a murderer. He would see himself on trial, vainly trying to bribe judges and lawyers while the courtroom rocked with laughter. And he would see himself walking toward a gallows rope on a pathway paved with money and the bones of his victims.

He shuddered now, wishing he could take a little walk, escape from this sixty-room prison and its electronically filtered air. But it was July, and the ragweed on the mainland was in ferocious bloom. Trees were casting their pollen into the wind. Flowers sprayed the stuff like hoses. The founder and only member of the Achievers of the New Order was a prisoner in his own fortress.

The intercom on his desk beeped. Shelmont leaned over and thumbed the talk switch. "What?"

"Manning's back again," his secretary said. "Do you want to see him?"

"Only if he's made progress."

"He says he needs to see you."

"All right. Did he shave his head yet?"

"Doesn't look like it."

"Shit. Put a towel over his head or something. If I sneeze once, I'll have his throat cut."

"He's on the way."

Shelmont slumped wearily in his leather-padded chair. Whenever someone came into the office, they invariably carried pollen with them. The damn paper capes didn't work for shit. The time was fast approaching when he would have to wear a spacesuit if he were to survive. What kind of a life would that be?

He stared across the gleaming expanse of his oaken desktop at the sterile steel walls, seeing his own vague reflection in them, a man approaching thirty but feeling like a hundred. This place was beginning to seem like a cage. Perhaps it was time to find a new island, build a new home, burn this one to the ground and sow the land with salt.

He clutched his head with his hands. Where were these crazy thoughts coming from?

The door slid open with an annoying squeak, and there stood Manning, a huge man in a brown tissue-paper poncho with his big feet sticking out underneath. He had wrapped another poncho around his head like a large turban.

"Get in and shut the fucking door," Shelmont snapped.

Manning leapt inside and the door squeaked shut.

Shelmont sneezed. "Shit! All right, what the hell is it?"

"He can't take much more," Manning said. He massaged his right bicep. "And my arm's getting tired."

"My arm's getting tired," Shelmont mimicked in a high, pansy voice. "My poor little arm." He jumped to his feet. "Screw you and your arm, Manning! I want results, do you hear me? I'll cut both of your fucking arms off if I have to!"

Manning rolled his eyes wearily, as if to say he had been through this before. "Don't blow a gasket, boss. I'm just here to say Vandevere's had enough."

"Never!" Shelmont shrieked. "I want him begging for mercy! I want him crawling on the floor! He's going to kiss my feet and beg me to bribe him! And you know what I'll do when he does? Know what I'll do?"

Manning raised his eyebrows.

"I'll kick him in the face," Shelmont screamed. He jumped away from the desk and began kicking at nothing. His hair fell across his eyes. "In the face!" he screamed, brushing it aside. "Right in the puss! Ha-ha! *Achoo*! Shit!"

He clutched his head again, reeling, sneezing. He stumbled backward and fell into his chair. For no reason at all tears sprang into his eyes and he felt sure he must weep. There was pressure on him, too much pressure. A lesser man would crack like a ripe nut.

"Okay," he said, forcing himself to be calm. He placed his hands flat on the desk, assembling himself. "State your case."

"Huh?"

"Give me the facts."

"Right. I've beat Vandevere to holy shit. He's got a busted nose, busted ribs, maybe a broken arm. His eyes are swollen all the way shut. He doesn't have any front teeth left at all. He's been bleeding out his ears. The whole damn basement floor is red. It stinks like a slaughterhouse down there. He even shit himself, I think."

Shelmont grinned. "He did, huh? Hah! Now we're getting somewhere."

Manning shook his head. "He's dying on us, boss. I mean, a man can only take so much." He looked down at his hands, and a brief expression of regret appeared on his face. "There isn't any skin left on his back. I've ruined two rubber hoses on him. I had to start on his legs."

He looked up and sighed. "It's making me sick to my stomach, boss."

"Pussy!" Shelmont shouted. "Pussy pussy pussy! Vandevere's faking, can't you tell? He's a cop, and a tough one. He's playing on your sympathies. Don't give in, Manning, my boy. Don't give in!"

Manning squirmed. "So what now?"

"We continue the treatment, of course. You do remember the last special project, don't you? That federal agent?"

Manning nodded. "He was easy."

"And his leg is nicely healing up while he basks in the sun on Tahiti. Picture Vandevere that way, Manning. Picture him in a chaise lounge on some faraway beach, sipping mint juleps while he mends. We'll pay him back for this inconvenience, you know. For every tooth he's lost, I'll pay dental bills plus pain-and-suffering expenses. You know me, Manning. I am a kind and generous man."

Manning gave him an uneasy smile. "That you are, boss."

"Right. So go back down and work Vandevere over a few more times. Crush his nuts in a vise if you have to. Make him choke on his own blood. He'll crack. Believe me, he'll crack."

"And if he doesn't?"

Shelmont narrowed his eyes. "Then we'll kill him. Kill him, kill him, kill him."

"When?"

Shelmont shrugged. "I don't know. I'm tired of fooling with him. Tonight, we'll say. Midnight tonight. If he won't join us by then, we'll kill him tonight. Feed him to the fucking sharks, too."

"There aren't no sharks in Lake Michigan, boss."

"Then I'll buy some, Manning. I'll buy a dozen of them if I have to. I can buy anything I want, anybody I want. Don't ever forget that."

"Right, boss."

"Now get the fuck out of here. *Achoo!*"

Manning left. Shelmont dropped his head tiredly into his hands. His heart was pounding and his lungs ached. It was all just too much. Someday he would buy the world and build a million planes to spray it all with herbicide, agent orange, or something. He would kill every single plant on the planet. And then he would be free.

But first there was this matter of Larry Vandevere to settle. Tonight, by midnight, one way or the other. And if he chose to die, then he would die.

Shelmont sneezed once more, then went back to the window. Already he was getting used to the idea of committing a federal offense. And it didn't feel so bad, once he got used to it. He knew he would never be caught, and if he were, there would be the simple matter of bribing a judge or intimidating a jury.

He stared out the window at the hazy orange sun that was sinking into the horizon, beginning to cheer up at last.

"I think we've timed it about right," Calvin Steeples said to his copilot, nine-year-old Missy Vandevere.

She checked her watch. Her flight helmet canted over her eyes and she had to push it back. "Nine forty-five, Chief. What's our ATE?"

"ATE?"

"I thought that's what you said a minute ago."

"Oh." Calvin chuckled. "That's ETA. Estimated time of arrival. And it's ten o'clock, that's our ETA."

"Roger, Captain."

Luke, crouched in the space between the pilot's seats, laughed out loud. Missy was loving this. After being cooped up in the cabin all this time, it was no wonder. When they'd lifted off from Superstitions Base four hours ago, she squealed with delight. For a while in the air,

Calvin had let her hold the copilot's yoke and fly the C-47. She felt she was contributing something to the mission now. She was helping DFI save her daddy.

The vintage aircraft slid noisily through the darkening sky at twelve thousand feet, its silver skin tinged with orange from the dying light. In the cargo section, Ben, Jake, and Tran were involved in a game of cards to pass the time.

Luke had tried to catch a nap on the hard cargo floor but found it impossible. His heart was beating just a little too fast, his senses just a little too alert for sleep. Somewhere over Missouri, just when he thought he might nod off, they had flown through a summer storm cell and been tossed around a little. By then Chicago was only an hour away, and Luke had gotten up, stiff and cranky, to pace the floor and go over the mission one more time in his mind.

Piece of cake. DFI had done harder things than this a dozen times in the past. In just a few hours it would all be over with.

If things went right, of course. And didn't things always have a way of going just a little bit wrong?

His mind skipped back two years, to the Guatemalan mission that had gone so awry and nearly cost everyone their lives. That had been a bad one. So bad, in fact, that it had convinced him that foreign missions were best left to the Foreign Legion. They had limped home in this very plane with the wind whistling through the bullet holes in the fuselage, weak and exhausted, lucky to be in one piece after confronting the entire Guatemalan national guard at the airport in Jalapa.

But that was then and this was now. Shelmont didn't have a national guard, he had a couple dozen goons in clown suits. Shelmont didn't have a country, he had an island.

So what could go wrong?

Nothing. Luke told himself that again and again.

The FBI had taken a brief but aggressive interest in Shelmont after the publicity following his political debut. They had gone so far as to plant a mole and request a series of satellite recon photos from the CIA's super-snooper satellite, the HK-14. The mole revealed that Shelmont was pretty much a harmless nut. Sure, his guys carried SMGs, but Shelmont had met all the necessary BATF requirements, so they let him have his fun. The HK-14 revealed an island roughly triangular in shape with a huge mansion located near the center, and a smaller hired-hands barracks on the eastern shore. A dock was built onto the western shore to handle boat traffic. Infrared photography showed that raw sewage was being piped from the mansion straight into Lake Michigan, but who really cared?

In short order the FBI withdrew its mole and closed down the investigation. They had gathered reams of materials in a few weeks time. Then they dumped it into the computer, where it sat untouched until Tran pulled it out.

Luke wondered at the speed with which the investigation shut down. It didn't take a genius to see that somebody's palm got greased. A political malcontent with a small army was allowed to conduct operations two miles from Chicago. It wasn't kosher. Somehow it just wasn't kosher. Somebody had been bought.

Luke checked his own watch now. "Missy," he said, "how would you like to watch three grown men paint their faces?"

"Really?" She looked at him, wrinkling her nose.

"Yeah. Go back there and tell Ben and Tran it's time to begin the festivities. I'll be there in a minute."

"Okay." She took the flight helmet off her head and set it on the floor, then wriggled past Luke.

"Cute kid," Calvin remarked when she was gone.

"Sure is. Do you have the mission profile straight?"

"Straight as an arrow, Luke."

"Good. We'll be counting on you."

"Have I ever let you down before?"

Luke smiled. "I recall a certain Guatemalan episode . . ."

"So I got a little nervous." Calvin rolled his eyes. "How was I to know there were trees at the end of the runway? It was dark."

"Everybody shit when you screamed."

"Yeah?" Calvin laughed. "Hell, *I* shit when I screamed. Not to worry this time, though."

"Okay." Luke stared out the windshield into the twilight. Past the C-47's nose, the lights of Chicago sparkled on the eastern horizon. "We'll be ready to jump on your signal, Cal." He patted his shoulder. "See you on the beach."

"Roger. And send Jake up here, will you? I might need help spotting the island."

Luke went aft, passing Jake, who was already on the way. Ben and Tran had their camouflage sticks out and were striping their faces with black and green while Missy stared at them, openmouthed.

"You look like sick tigers," she said, and giggled.

"Wait till you see me jump out that door," Tran said. "I'll *be* a sick tiger."

They laughed as they prepared for the jump. Each man was wearing flame-retardant black fatigues, a CO_2 flotation vest, a dark boonie hat, an assault vest, and a black pistol belt with six ammo pouches. Each wore his pistol of choice across his chest: Luke had a Smith & Wesson .357; Ben his police revolver; and Tran a Sig-Sauer 9-mm automatic. Hooked in the weapons rack opposite the door were two M16s and Luke's traditional M203, the combination M16 rifle and 40-mm grenade launcher he favored. Ben had a Marine Corps knife strapped to his leg; Tran had a large WWI trench knife sticking out of one boot. For each man a padded black bag containing night-vision goggles, extra ammo, and special equipment rested by the door.

For communication, each assault vest had a small battery transceiver tucked in the breast pocket, snugged down by a Velcro strip. A thin wire ran from this into each man's fatigue shirt, up past his collar, and under his hat, ending in an earphone and wire boom mike. On the ground these would be activated, enabling the team to speak to each other. Luke found it preferable to the bulky military walkie-talkies, and far more reliable. On jumps, especially night jumps, walkie-talkies often didn't survive the tumble to the ground.

They helped each other into their parachutes. Through the porthole windows the bright lights of downtown Chicago at night gleamed, and the C-47 began to lurch a little as it collided with the warm air rising from the city.

Luke buckled Missy into one of the canvas-webbed seats across from the sliding door, with an admonition not to get out of it for any reason. When the red light above the door winked on, he cranked the door handle and slid it open into the night.

The brightness of Chicago was split neatly in half below, with utter darkness on the right where the land ended and the water of Lake Michigan began. Warm wind blasted through the door, pummeling Tran, who leaned out to take in the scenery. Calvin had descended to one thousand feet, as arranged, and cut the engines down to a muted rumble. Gliding in at this altitude, their passage over Guiles Island should go unnoticed.

"Okay, Ben," Luke said. "We'll pass the western shore first."

Ben slung his M16 and his equipment bag across his chest and positioned himself at the door, spread-eagle, holding on to the aluminum frame. The wind rippled his clothes into crazy shapes. He had exchanged his boonie hat temporarily for a nonreflective crash helmet that he would discard on the ground. He looked back at Luke and gave him a thumbs-up.

"Going to say it?" Luke shouted above the wind.

"Would I be a heretic if I did?"

"Not in my book."

"Will they hear me on the ground?"

"Not a chance."

The red light above the door went out, and the green one flashed on.

Ben jumped. His voice trailed after him as he fell: "*Geronimo*!"

The light went red again. Luke tucked his boonie hat in the thigh pocket of his fatigues and put on a crash helmet, then picked up his gear and stood at the door. On the wind he could smell the city and the deep, fishy aroma of the lake. Distantly below, Shelmont's mansion passed into view, brightly lit by floodlights. He turned and gave Missy a thumbs-up. She returned it, wide-eyed with excitement.

The light went green. Luke hurled himself out with his arms clasped together over his chest and his feet locked together. After three seconds he gave the rip cord a yank and heard his parachute flap behind him as it unfolded. There was a crisp snap overhead, and his harness gave him a tremendous upward jerk as the black-camouflaged parachute unfurled and caught his weight.

He floated down, examining the landscape. His course was taking him beyond the bright mansion to the darkness of the northern half of the island. The C-47 droned innocuously overhead, sounding no different than any commercial aircraft making an approach toward O'Hare or Midway. A quarter moon hung in the sky, casting weak light, making the grass below look gray. A slight easterly breeze pushed Luke gently sideways.

He hit the ground near the shore without losing his balance and immediately reeled in his chute, collapsing it. He wriggled out of his harness and hastily rolled the entire unit into a flat ball, then took off his crash helmet and replaced it with his boonie.

He lay flat on his stomach, breathing hard, watching.

After a moment he hooked his earphone over his ear and adjusted the wire mike at his lips. He turned the transceiver on, then whispered into the mike.

"Ben?"

He waited, straining to hear.

"Come in, Ben. I need to know if you're in one piece."

Nothing.

He pounded a fist on the grass. Already something had gone wrong.

It started right after Ben shouted "Geronimo!"

His chute unfurled with a low *whoofing* sound instead of the usual bright snap of nylon against air. He felt himself jerked to the left. Looking up, he could see that the parachute cords extending up to the right had twisted around each other, forming a thick rope instead of a well-spaced net. The chute itself flapped and rippled, collapsed on one side.

He looked down at the ground rushing up to meet him. Wind whistled in his ears. He was drifting west, past the white band of Guiles Island's shoreline and toward the deep black of the open lake. That, at least, was lucky. He guessed he was falling at twice, maybe three times, the normal rate. To hit the ground at this speed would mean two broken legs at the very least.

Working the tangled cords with his hands, bicycling his legs to keep upright, Ben hit the water sixty feet from shore, sending a geyser of water sparkling up into the moonlight.

The perpetually cold water of Lake Michigan swallowed him, blotting out light and sound. He wriggled free of his chute and kicked away from it before pulling the ring on his flotation vest.

It filled instantly, and he bobbed to the surface, blowing and gasping. On impact his M16 had flipped up and cracked him across the face, and now he could feel a warm trickle of blood where the bolt release had gouged his forehead. He dog-paddled toward shore, thankful that a little cut was the only price he'd had to pay for such a botched jump.

A flashlight snapped on in the darkness ahead of him, casting a thin white beam. He heard the distinctive click of a weapon being cocked. The beam swept across the water, searching.

Ben's heart sank as the light caught him full in the face and stayed there.

"Come on out slow," someone growled.

His feet found the rocky lake bottom after a moment and he walked, pushing up out of the water. The light continued to blind him as he clambered onto the shore.

"Well, what the hell we got here?" the man said, inspecting him as water sluiced out of his clothes. "Some kind of Mexican sky diver?"

Ben held his tongue. On the grass behind the man he could make out the form of a golf cart.

The light snapped off. "I've got you covered, so don't even think about making a move." The man backed up to the cart. He reached between the seats and withdrew a walkie-talkie. He clicked it on.

Ben could sense the mission crumbling before it had a chance to start.

He crouched slightly and pulled his Marine Corps knife out of its sheath.

"Base?" the man said. He shook the walkie-talkie. "Hey, base?"

Ben lunged at him, swinging the knife in a flat arc at waist level.

The blade sliced deeply from right to left through the man's stomach.

In a swift second move, Ben plunged his left hand through the cut into the man's abdomen. With a jerk he shoveled his guts out onto the grass.

The man emitted a long, mournful sigh. A gray rope of large intestine still unwound slowly out of the gaping slash in his stomach, coiling in a wet pile on the grass. He looked at it with wide and mystified eyes. His knees unhinged, and he spilled over onto his face.

Ben scrubbed his bloody hand on his wet fatigue pants, breathing through his mouth. The smell of human bowels hung in the air like a cloud of gas.

The walkie-talkie hissed. "Base here. What's up?"

Ben picked it up and threw it into the lake.

Chapter 12

Tran Cao had problems of his own.

Drifting slowly down over the eastern rim of the island, the last man out, he could make out the target of his drop below: the squat, two-story wooden barracks that housed Shelmont's cadre of island guards. Calvin had flashed the green light at the perfect moment; this jump would win medals for accuracy. And therein lay the problem.

He was floating down right onto the roof.

He squirmed in his harness, trying desperately to tug the chute sideways. The gentle breeze off the lake carried him eastward, the direction he no longer wanted to go. His feet clipped the peak of the gabled roof as he passed, slowing him. The chute collapsed and dumped him hard on the sloping shingles.

He began a rolling slide down the roof, his arms and feet flailing and thumping, while parachute cords tangled themselves around his chest and neck. He clawed the pebbly surface, erasing the skin from his fingertips, tearing holes in his fatigues at the knees. At the drop-off he reached wildly as he fell and caught the edge of the aluminum gutter.

It jerked under the sudden burden of his weight into a broad V-shape. The metal groaned and popped against its moorings.

For a moment he hung there while his chute floated dreamily past like a dark ghost.

Through the white siding of the wall, inches in front of his face, he could hear men talking. A foot to his right, a four-pane window cast light into the night.

Would have been funny, he thought, looking at the window. *Would have been real funny if I was hanging in front of* that.

He swung a leg up and hooked his heel into the gutter. It creaked and muttered. He brought himself up, straining against his weight and the drag of the collapsed chute. Balancing on his knees, he reached up and caught the lip of the roof. He hauled himself up, turned, and sat down on the slope with his legs dangling over the edge.

Working quickly, he pulled his chute up hand over hand. He wriggled out of the harness and entanglement of cords and shoved the chute back into its pack as best he could, then set it aside.

That done, he unslung his M16 and cautiously pulled the charging handle back. When he heard a round snap up into place, he eased the handle forward, then tapped the forward assist with the heel of his hand to make sure the bolt had seated.

All the while he waited for the consequence of his noisy landing.

You could not, he reasoned, fall on top of somebody's house like a sack of bricks and expect to go unnoticed. Someone would hear, and someone would come out. And you could bet they would not be looking for Santa Claus.

Santa Cao, maybe. Tran grinned to himself. American traditions could sometimes be a real chuckle.

The consequence he had expected came a moment later.

Four men burst out of the back door two floors beneath Tran's dangling feet, all carrying Uzi SMGs and looking very nervous. They stared skyward, whispering to each other.

Tran drew his feet up, cocking his knees under his chin.

They fanned out across the grass, nearly disappearing in the dark as the door swung shut behind them. Tran took his helmet off and set it on the roof. He unzipped his equipment bag and brought out his night-vision goggles. Setting them over his eyes, he fingered the switch between the eyepieces. The night crystallized into a field of foggy green, like an underwater world. Almost as an afterthought, he set his earphone and mike in place and turned on the transceiver in the breast pocket of his vest.

Luke's voice whispered immediately in his ear.

"Tran? Come in."

Tran reached up and slowly tapped the wire mike with a fingernail three times.

"Repeat if you can," Luke said.

Tran did it again. The men below were staring up at the roof. With the moon shining in the western sky, this eastern side of the roof was dark. But was it dark enough? Tran watched them, four green men with dark dots for eyes.

"Ben's not responding," Luke said. "Are you in place?"

Tran tapped three times.

"Sit quiet for five minutes. If Ben doesn't make contact by then, we assume he's out and go to Plan B."

Tran frowned, then smiled grimly. For Luke there was never Plan B. There were too many variables involved in any operation to judge a plan's success or failure by the emergence of a single unexpected factor, such as Ben's silence. Luke and Tran might well switch to Plan B, only to find that Ben was still following Plan A. That could be disastrous. The only Plan B that existed for Deadly Force

Incorporated was this simple standing order: Do whatever your instincts tell you.

One of the men pointed up at Tran. The others looked.

Tran brought the muzzle of his M16 to bear on him. With his thumb he clicked the selector to full auto.

His role in the mission was simple: Keep the guards in their barracks. If that meant killing a few of them, fine. If that meant killing them all, then fine again. DFI had never been known for its charity.

One of them bent down and picked up a rock. He threw it at the roof. It hit the shingles to Tran's right and bounced, skittered over the gable, and was gone on the other side.

"Hit anything?" one of them called out.

"Damned if I know. I can't see shit."

"Anybody got a flashlight?"

"Hold on a minute, I'll get one."

One green figure hurried to the door. Through the goggles, Tran's eyes were seared by a wash of brilliant emerald light as the door opened.

"I'll bet it was one of them UFO jobs," someone below said. "Or a meteor."

Another laughed. "It was just a sea gull flying into one of the windows, asshole. They do it all the time."

"Not that loud," the other said. "I was laying on my bunk and heard it real good. Something landed on the roof. Probably on the other side."

"Somebody's already checking the other side."

The door opened again. Tran averted his eyes this time.

"Okay, shine it up there."

A beam sprang into existence and swept the roof. Tran made himself as small as he could get.

"There!"

The beam swept back and caught him in a circle of light. He estimated he had given Luke about one quiet minute of the requested five. He would, unfortunately, have to make do with what he got.

"What the hell is it?" one of them cried.

"Biggest fucking bird I ever saw."

"Look at its eyes! It's a Martian!"

"Martian, my ass. Watch this."

An Uzi was raised.

Tran pulled the trigger in a short burst, making mental apologies to Luke. The M16 spit green fire.

One bullet caught the man raising the Uzi in the shoulder. His left arm tore free of his body in a spray of green blood and pinwheeled into the air. He wobbled on his feet and fell sideways, screaming. His arm thumped down on the grass behind him.

Tran swiveled the M16 and cut down the others before they could react.

In the barracks beneath him, men began to shout.

A moment later the rest of the cadre started pouring out.

"Shit," Luke muttered when the noise began.

He got to his feet. The mansion was a distant point of light, the noise of Tran's firefight a dull, intermittent hammering to the east of it, echoed in his earphone. He set off at a trot, unslinging his rifle and holding it by the carrying handle as he ran. With his free hand he opened his poplin bag and brought out his night-vision goggles.

Guiles Island became a green shadowland as he put them on. He glanced around with his new vision, seeing only a treeless expanse of well-kept grass, crisscrossed by dim impressions of tires. But for the lack of trees it gave him the feeling of being on a vast, rolling golf course. He had to give Shelmont credit for one thing—he had turned what the FBI report called a "mosquito-infested pit" into some nice acreage.

Too bad he might not live past tonight to enjoy it.

Dazzling light appeared suddenly to his right, bursting out of nowhere. Luke flopped down.

It was a golf cart, zipping soundlessly across the grass on fat balloon tires with two intent-looking men carrying Uzis sitting inside. A powerful searchlight was mounted on the front, throwing an unbearable green beam. They drove directly toward Luke, headed for the eastern shore where Tran was making so much noise.

Luke rolled to the side, tearing his goggles off his head. In normal light now, he could make out the searchlight bearing down on him, and see the dim shadows of the two men sitting behind it.

One shouted something. The cart skidded to a stop. The beam swiveled, probing the darkness like a skeletal, white finger. They began shouting at each other.

"I tell you, I saw something!"

"So what? Can't you hear what's going on?"

The cart lurched forward.

"Stop, dammit! There! See?"

Luke's first shot blew the searchlight apart with a noisy explosion of glass.

He slipped his goggles back on as the cart skidded to a fresh stop and two Uzis opened up like chattering thunder. Dirt and grass burst up around him as the ground was stitched with two dozen instant holes.

He rolled again and fired full auto.

The night-vision goggles, capturing and magnifying the available light, presented a clear, if greenish, picture as the two men jittered and flopped in their seats like victims of a sudden gangland massacre.

The golf cart rocked and bucked; a front tire blew with a hissing explosion.

Luke let off the trigger. The driver slumped forward with blood draining out of nine pencil-thick holes in his chest. The other leaned slowly sideways, staring ahead with bulging eyes, tipping out. His stomach had been blown fully open and was spilling some kind of liquid into his lap. He thumped to the ground like something made of soft rubber.

Luke got to his feet and went to the cart.

"Sorry about the tire," he said, and yanked the driver out. Chunks of him remained stuck to the bullet-riddled back of the vinyl seat; Luke brushed them away before dropping his bag in the back and sitting down behind the wheel. He tried the pedal, and the cart surged forward with a small electric whine. The blown tire rattled and thumped, jerking the steering wheel back and forth.

"Piece of shit," Luke muttered.

"What?" Tran barked in his ear.

"Ah, he speaks at last," Luke said. "You sure are making a lot of noise over there."

"No shit?" His M16 rattled as he spoke. "I thought you said there were only a couple dozen guys here."

"How many are you engaging?"

"At least thirty. I'm on the roof."

Luke frowned. "Bad spot, Frags. Better get down."

"Easier to say than to do, Luke. They're running me all over the place, everywhere but down."

"Have they gone upstairs to shoot through the roof yet?"

Tran groaned. "No, but they'll think of it soon enough. I hate to say it, but we may have a situation on our hands. This is more than we bargained for."

"Did your bag survive the drop?"

"Yeah."

"Then use some heavy stuff on them. Just don't let them get underneath you."

"Okay. No time for talk now. Bye bye."

"Roger. Scream if you die, so I'll know."

"Very funny, Luke."

Luke guided the cart up a gentle rise, exchanging his nearly spent twenty-round magazine for a fresh one from an ammo pouch as he drove. When he reached the top of the rise, he stopped to gain his bearings on the faraway pinpoint of light that was Shelmont's house.

Other golf carts were racing across the plain spread out before him, each preceded by the brilliant shaft of a searchlight, each homing in on the eastern shore of the island.

Bad tactics, Luke thought. You never gather all your forces to one spot. You guard the perimeter in expectation of a second thrust.

He was the second thrust, he knew. And Shelmont's forces were paving the way for him. Unfortunately for Tran, they were also bunching up on his location. That would make things even tougher for the little Vietnamese.

Luke mashed the pedal to the floor, determined to lighten the load for Tran if he could. With his ruined tire flapping, he sped down the slope to intercept a cart coming in from the right. As it cut in front of him, he opened fire on the two startled occupants, lifting them out of their seats as if pulled by invisible wires.

One of them cartwheeled through the air and flopped down in front of Luke's speeding cart, giving it a tremendous bounce as he rolled underneath.

This sudden burst of firepower caught the attention of the other guards. They turned, circling back, their searchlights probing the night.

Luke fired again as they approached. The cart he was targeting swerved in a wild circle, tipped up on its side, and overturned. Two men were thrown out, but one of them got up again, firing wildly at nothing in his panic.

Luke raked him with a short burst. The left side of the man's head blew apart, fanning wet chunks of brain across the grass behind him. His legs scissored and he fell.

Now two carts were coming straight at Luke, locking

him in the jittering beams of their searchlights. Fire blossomed simultaneously from the barrels of four Uzis.

Luke ducked, swerving his cart left, out of their light. Bullets punched through his cart's fiberglass body with small clacking noises, clanging loudly as they struck metal parts. The cart developed a sudden electric wheeze and began to slow.

The two carts turned, homing in on Luke's rear. Three more approached from the right to join them. Their lights became blinding green spots through the goggles.

He reached back into his bag and fished out a 40-mm high-explosive grenade. As his cart shuddered to a stop, he cracked the breech of the grenade launcher portion of his M203, jammed the HE round inside, and swiveled it shut.

He jumped out and crouched in front of the cart. Bullets pounded the rear as he aimed directly at the oncoming lights.

He pulled the grenade launcher's trigger. Even with their searchlights, Shelmont's guards had no idea what he had done. They proceeded on, closing the distance, firing steadily.

The grenade slammed into the front-most cart, punching through the thick fiberglass bonnet.

A second later it exploded in a geyser of light and sound, breaking the cart in half and hurling its occupants fifteen feet into the sky. Two other carts to the right of it turned over, their lights wheeling in crazy circles.

Luke stood up and emptied the rest of his magazine on the men who had been thrown to the ground.

The two remaining golf carts spun hastily around under this hail of fire and headed away. Luke jammed a fresh magazine into the rifle, went down on one knee, and drew a quick sight picture on one of the driver's heads. With his own cart out of action, it was now time to procure another, and the only ones available were either overturned or blown to shit. Besides, he thought, it would be a refreshing change to drive one that had four good tires.

His shot cleaved a deep ravine through the driver's skull, throwing him forward and out of the cart.

The rider grabbed for the wheel with both hands, looking back over his shoulder with an expression that was, even through the foggy green of Luke's goggles, clearly one of pure terror.

Luke shot him cleanly through the neck. His head snapped around, then lolled out of sight.

The cart rolled to a stop.

It grew quiet then, save for the distant noise of gunfire to the east. The last occupied cart and its two men rolled swiftly away, no longer heading for Tran's position, no longer heading, in Luke's estimation, anywhere at all. Shelmont couldn't pay these guys enough for this kind of action. Like most wise mercenaries, they were pulling back to ask themselves if the pay was worth the risk.

Luke got his equipment bag out of the dead cart and went to the newly vacated one. He shoved the dead man out and dropped his bag on the passenger seat.

In the east he heard the rumble of a grenade exploding.

"Get 'em, Frags," he whispered, wishing he could be there to help. But there were other matters to take care of now.

"Ben?" he said loudly into his microphone. "You with us yet, Ben?"

No reply. A deep chill of worry passed through his mind. Without Ben there was no easy way off this island. Without Ben this piece-of-cake mission suddenly got twice as hard.

From here on out it would be Plan B all the way. And Plan B never seemed to be quite as good as Plan A.

He drove toward the brightly lit expanse of Shelmont's mansion, wondering what the hell had gone wrong.

· · ·

Ben Sanchez was wondering the same thing himself.

After gutting the man who had captured him coming out of the water, Ben had made his way south, following the shoreline toward the dock Luke's FBI satellite photo had shown existed to handle Shelmont's supply and pleasure boats. His transceiver was a broken pile of plastic in his vest pocket; apparently his M16 had damaged more than just his face when he hit the water. His delicate night-vision goggles had not been made for use underwater and refused to function no matter how many times he shook them out.

Disgusted, he gave up and shoved them back in the bag draped over his chest. The light of the quarter moon in the western sky would have to be enough.

He stayed on the grass, away from the band of white rock that formed the beach. To his right Chicago was a distant, colorful splash, two miles across the water. The moon sparkled on the lake, and gentle waves surged against the shore, loud enough to mask the whisper of his feet through the grass. He walked bent over in a crouch, sweeping his head left and right, not willing to be caught unawares again. His wet clothes squished quietly as he moved.

Three hundred yards from the point he had exited the water, he saw a brief pinpoint of orange light in the darkness ahead. He went down on his haunches, straining to see.

The light swung upward in a short arc. It glowed brighter, then dimmed.

Ben nodded. Someone had decided it was time for a smoke and was enjoying his cigarette standing at the shore looking out across the water toward Chicago. Doubtless someone wishing he were there instead of here, where the boredom of guarding this quiet island had to be excruciating.

Ben went down on his stomach and crept closer. Soon he could make out the form of the man, sitting where the grass ended and the rocks began, his knees tucked up under his chin, the glowing cigarette in his hand. A few yards behind him sat a dark and quiet golf cart. Against the whiteness of the vinyl seat Ben could see another man. His chin was on his chest; he appeared to be dozing.

Ben angled toward the cart. As he drew up beside it, he could see a distant puddle of light on the shore another two hundred yards away. It was the dock, stretching out over the water, lighted by a line of poles that ran the length of it. Two boats were visible from this angle. Two boats, and at least three golf carts with men sitting in them.

It looked like things were going to be tough from here on out.

Ben unsheathed his Marine Corps knife once again, going up on his knees beside the sleeping man.

He poised the tip of the black blade under the man's jaw and wished his soul a safe passage to the afterlife.

He thrust the knife through the side of the man's neck into his spinal cord. Just as quickly he jerked the blade out. A thin line of blood trickled out of the slit.

Ben had purposefully avoided his jugular vein and carotid artery. Splashing blood would have alerted the other guard.

Sleeping peacefully, the man died. His arms, which were crossed over his stomach, slid apart and dropped to his sides.

Ben got to his feet, still crouched low, and padded softly to the man smoking the cigarette. He stood behind him for a silent moment, looking down at the top of his head. This one had a bald spot. Ben wondered momentarily what kind of man he was, how this man of all the billions in the world should happen to be at this spot to die. Did he have a wife, kids, a pet dog? Was he divorced, lonely, nice, mean? Did he worry that his smoking might be harmful to his health? Did he help little old ladies across the street? Or was he a cruel and heartless bastard?

None of it mattered. Ben felt a quick moment of intense sadness. His Apache's reverence for life was deep and genuine. But his instinct for survival was just as strong.

He grabbed a handful of the man's remaining hair, jerking his head viciously backward. At the same instant he slashed his knife across the exposed throat, peeling it wide open.

The gout of blood was immediate and gigantic. The man clapped his hands to his throat as if to stop the flood. Blood washed over his cigarette, extinguishing it with a hiss. Severed cartilage made wet clicking noises as he tried in vain to breathe. His legs shot straight out as he went into a jittering death throe.

Ben released his hair, letting him stretch out backward, and watched him die. His eyes were bright and bulging in the moonlight, full of terror and misery. The smell of blood was in the air, a smell like warm seawater. He jerked and flopped.

Twenty seconds later he died.

Ben bent down and slid his eyes shut.

It was at that moment that Tran Cao opened fire from his perch on the roof, two miles away on the opposite side of the island.

Ben dropped down, waiting to see what the reaction at the dock would be. He heard distant startled voices. He heard the metal click of Uzis being cocked. Four figures in red pants and black shirts hurried into two of the golf carts and sped away into the dark heart of the island.

One man remained behind. He began to pace nervously along the width of the dock, his feet thumping on the planking. Ben saw him spin in a hasty circle, waving his Uzi, then slap angrily at the back of his neck.

Mosquito. And one jumpy guard.

Ben sheathed his knife, unslung his M16, and sighted in on him. It occurred to him that this single shot might bring the other guards hurrying back. That wouldn't do any good. It was his task to commandeer one of Shelmont's boats, not spend all night in a firefight.

He hooked the sling back over his shoulder and waded out into the water. When it was chest-deep, he started south again.

In five minutes he had pushed to within ten yards of the dock. The sounds of battle had grown closer, and once Ben heard the unmistakable whump of one of Luke's 40-mm grenades, somewhere in the center of the island. Things seemed to be proceeding not quite according to plan.

According to Luke this was to be a silent insertion, a surgical procedure carried out with surgical precision.

Apparently things were falling apart all over the place.

Ben came to the dock and paused behind one of the thick cement pilings that supported the wooden structure. The guard paced back and forth above him. Moonlight winked off his shiny shoes as he passed. Ben worked his way under the dock, which stood a foot above the water, and emerged at the other side.

Now the guard had stopped pacing and was cocking his head from side to side as if listening. The noise of gunfire had ebbed after the grenade explosion. To Ben it sounded like the action in the center of the island had ended; hopefully Luke had come out the victor in that engagement.

The noise from Tran's position continued. Ben heard the sharp bang of a fragmentation grenade exploding—Tran had brought out the heavy artillery.

Ben pulled himself hand over hand along the dock, out toward deep water. A huge white boat sat imposingly on the water near the end of the dock, doubtless Shelmont's yacht. On the other side a smaller powerboat bobbed against its ropes. Halfway to the end of the dock, Ben hoisted himself slowly out of the water, keeping his eyes fixed on the guard, who had resumed his pacing. When he was fully out and his clothes had drained, he took his knife in his hand once again and crept toward him.

The guard's concern was focused on the land—even as he turned in his pacing and his eyes swept past Ben, a crouching figure fully visible under the light, it failed to register in his mind. Twice he simply stopped with his back to Ben and stared off across the island.

Ben moved inexorably closer to him, and when the guard stopped for the third time to listen to the sounds of Tran's continuing battle, Ben was upon him.

It was not as clean as Ben hoped.

He clamped his left arm around the guard's head from behind, drawing it back and sideways to expose the right side of his throat. He positioned his knife under the hinge of the man's jaw and plunged the blade home, intending to sever his spinal cord and kill him instantly, the way he had killed the sleeping man.

Instead he felt the tip of his blade glance off bone, and heard the wet crunch as the metal sliced uselessly against a vertebra.

The spinal cord was intact when the man jerked away and began to scream.

Chapter 13

Jonathan Shelmont was having a sudden and excruciating attack of nerves about then.

Inside the air-filtered portion of his mansion, the part protected by air-lock doors and pollen-free antiseptic walls, the sounds of battle drifted through like distant drumming, disturbing him as he watched the ten o'clock news on giant-screen television. From the comfort of his plastic-covered sofa he clicked the TV off and cocked his head to listen. In his red silk smoking jacket he was the perfect picture of serene wealth, a man posing attentively for his portrait.

His heart jumped in his chest. Once before, in April of last year, one of his guards had gotten roaring drunk over a game of cards and shot up the barracks, causing quite a commotion and forcing Shelmont to ban drinking on the island. In a way it made him nervous to have all these peasants wandering around with machine guns, but like many other things, he had gotten used to it. It was necessary, at least until a perfect world was established and the peasants were no longer allowed anything at all.

But now, listening to the steady clamor of shooting, Jonathan Shelmont knew something far more deadly was happening.

There was shooting to the east, and now to the west. The mansion was surrounded by distant gunfire. And Jonathan Shelmont was in the middle of a battle zone, sitting in his red silk smoking jacket in the middle of a battle zone.

What he had secretly feared was happening at last.

The peasants were revolting.

Mutiny on Guiles Island.

Fear washed over him in hot waves. They had lived too long in the shadow of his mansion and his money, lived too long in relative poverty while he basked in opulence. Secretly they had envied him; secretly they had hated him. In the privacy of their barracks, and while riding together on patrols, they had plotted against him.

His own men were out to murder Jonathan Shelmont and steal his money.

Loathing and hatred, always festering in his brain, flared brightly, blotting out reason and tempering his fear. They would storm the mansion, sure they would, they would storm the mansion and break down the doors, carrying torches like the rampaging villagers of some Frankenstein movie, intent on killing the tortured genius who had created the monster. Only Shelmont had not created a monster, he had created a vision and a dream.

And he would not see them killed. Not this way.

He jumped up, panting, already feeling a warm sheen of sweat on his body. He ran out of the TV room into the master bedroom, sliding and skating in his stocking feet on the polished steel floor, waving his arms for balance. He broke through into the dining room, where every day he ate his meals in solitude on a glass table. From there he came out on a hallway, which led to his office and his intercom. By the time he got to it and punched the button, he was screaming.

"Traitors!"

His night secretary's voice was bland. "Yes, Mr. Shelmont?"

"Are you one of them?" he shrieked. "Are you?"

"One of who, Mr. Shelmont?"

His face twisted into a knowing leer. "Go ahead, bitch," he snarled. "Play dumb!"

"Mr. Shelmont!"

"Get me a gun, if you're still with me. Prove your loyalty."

She hesitated for a long time then. Finally: "A gun?"

"Yes, damn you. Bang-bang. Get one for yourself and stand by my side to the end."

"Does that mean you want a gun, like, *now*?"

"Yes, for God's sake, yes! Can't you hear them shooting outside?"

"Sorry. I had my Walkman on."

"Peasants!" Spit flew from his lips. His face was becoming decidedly purple. "Morons! Imbeciles! Get me a goddamn gun! And lots of bullets!"

"Right away, sir."

Shelmont smashed the intercom off the desk and stalked around the office, fuming and cursing.

A few minutes later the door squeaked open. His secretary stood there in a paper poncho, carrying an Uzi.

He had his gun.

Luke was within fifty feet of the main gate, racing along the wrought-iron fence toward the brick guardhouse, when the guard there spotted him and opened fire. One bullet from the Uzi smashed against his M203's stock, shattering it into long shards and nearly jerking the rifle out of his hands.

Luke dived out of the cart and rolled in the grass, coming to rest in the prone firing position.

The guardhouse looked empty. Then a head poked up. Luke blew it off the man's shoulders. He slumped out the widow with a thick fountain of blood pulsing out of the ragged remains of his neck, his arms dangling to the ground.

Bent low, Luke ran to the gate and crouched behind one of the stone pillars that supported it. Through the wrought-iron bars he could see the front entrance to the mansion, a carapace supported by statues. It was lit with red, blue, and green floodlights.

One by one he shot them out. When the doorway was dark he dug his insulated wire cutters out of his bag and climbed the fence to dispose of the three strands there. That done, he vaulted over the fence and disappeared into the hedges that ringed the house.

A moment later a window to his right was flung open and someone leaned out. A Uzi spit fire toward the guardhouse, ejecting a stream of hot cartridge casings that tumbled into the bushes near Luke's feet. Bullets sparked and ricocheted uselessly off the stone structure. The headless body of the guard sprouted holes.

The Uzi fell silent and was withdrawn.

Luke heard the sounds of reloading. He stepped under the window, lifted his broken rifle over his head, went up on tiptoe, and stuck the barrel through. He pulled the trigger and swept the M203 back and forth, leaning his weight against its thrust.

Someone screamed inside. Someone thudded to the floor.

Luke drew it back down and popped the magazine out. Smoke drifted out of the receiver. He put in a fresh magazine with the familiar and somehow exhilarating burned-chemical smell of expended smokeless powder stinging his nostrils.

He pushed through the bushes, sidling to the front door. It was made of dark wood, exquisitely carved in some kind of Oriental motif, most decidedly imported. He reached out, made a fist, and pounded on it once.

The door burst into sudden rattling motion as bullets chewed through the wood in a hail of chips and splinters.

Luke ducked back, shielding his eyes until the storm had ended. When it had, Shelmont's imported door looked like it had been to the moon and back.

Luke counted the holes, his eyes darting swiftly. Thirty-plus. That meant two Uzis were behind it. Shelmont's men were packing twenty-round loads.

He swung his rifle up and blew the doorknob off with a six-round burst.

Now he heard voices inside. And the click of SMGs getting a quick reloading.

He waited until they were done.

He knocked again.

The door cracked and splintered in an explosion of sawdust, hammered to pieces from the inside by some very nervous guards. The torrent lasted four seconds, the time it takes to empty twenty rounds through the barrel of an Uzi.

Luke jumped in front of the door before they could reload. He kicked it open, saw two men in their peculiar pizza-boy suits through the fog of gunsmoke inside, and pulled his M203's trigger to unleash a fire storm of lead.

Nothing happened. He instinctively thumped the forward assist with the heel of his hand, hard enough to put a bruise there. He raked the trigger back, and again nothing happened. Hopelessly jammed. It would take a screwdriver and a lot of time to get the obstructed cartridge out. Something for Jake to do as he whiled away the hours.

The two guards had shrank back in fear and surprise. Now one of them realized what was happening and went ahead with his reloading, pulling a magazine out of a back pocket and slipping it up into an Uzi with one nervous hand. He butted it in place.

The other guard turned and stumbled away into the depths of the house.

The remaining guard leveled his Uzi at Luke's chest. A nervous but triumphant grin spread across his face.

Luke lunged at him just as he fired, dropping the useless M203 and yanking his revolver from the holster at his chest. Bullets shot past his ears as he dived wildly between the guard's legs, recovered, and turned to drill two point-blank holes through his spine.

The guard spun in a circle, his face contorted with agony, still firing crazily even as he died. Nine-millimeter bullets clipped the overhead chandelier, blowing it apart. Glass rattled down.

Luke sprinted after the other man, who had fled down a dim hallway that opened on a huge main parlor. This had to be Shelmont's imperial sitting room, Luke decided as he surveyed it. There were rows of portraits and photographs on the walls. He recognized the faces of Henry Ford, J. P. Morgan, John D. Rockefeller, and Joseph Kennedy, all wealthy, self-made men, all achievers of the highest sort. The biggest portrait of all, hanging in the center of the west wall, was of a young man with thinning brown hair and narrow, glinting blue eyes. The Big Achiever himself, then. His Majesty, Jonathan Shelmont.

There were lots of antiques in here, a large globe of the world in a wooden stand, a wet bar in the corner with crystal glasses stacked in a pyramid. To Luke's right, and perhaps strangest of all, someone had left their shoes sticking out under the drapes.

Luke smiled, shaking his head slightly. Terror will often drive men to do idiotic things. The drapes clearly showed the outline of the man hiding behind them; the drapes were quaking and shivering. The drapes were even uttering little gasps of fright.

"Gee, I guess nobody's here," Luke said loudly. "Perhaps I will shoot holes through the drapes to vent my anger at having found no one.''

The drapes gasped. The guard worked his way out of them like an actor trying to find his way through stage curtains. When he emerged, he was crying.

"Oh, God, mister, please," he wailed. Somewhere along the way he had dropped his Uzi, and now he raised his hands high over his head. "Don't kill me. I swear I ain't got no gun. See? So don't kill me."

"Where's Vandevere?" Luke snarled.

"Who?"

Luke clicked the .357's hammer back with his thumb. "Larry Vandevere. Take me to him."

"Oh, shit," the guard said miserably. "You're not going to believe this, but I don't know what you're talking about. I just work here, you know, guard the place. I don't know anything about anybody. I swear it."

Luke deliberated. This man was too terrified to be lying. And that raised again the question that had been bothering Luke for some time: What if Larry wasn't here? What then?

And, by the by, where was Ben? If they couldn't get off the island, there would be some very serious matters to deal with. Like the rest of Shelmont's guards, for one thing. Like the law, for another.

"Take me to Shelmont," he said.

"Yeah." The guard nodded enthusiastically. "That I can do. You bet. This way."

He led Luke through another series of rooms, down more hallways, and finally upstairs. They stopped at a polished steel door. The guard punched a button on the intercom panel set in the wall beside it.

"They have to clear us before we can get in," he said, giving Luke an apologetic grin. "Shelmont's a crazy son of a bitch."

After a long moment a woman replied, "What?"

Luke pressed the barrel of his revolver against the guard's neck. "Do it right," he whispered.

"Gilson here," the guard said. "I need to see Mr. Shelmont."

"I don't think you want to," she said. "He's flipped."

"It's urgent. Tell him that."

"Up to you. Hold on."

The guard, Gilson, turned to Luke. "Am I doing okay?"

"Just get us in there."

The woman came back on. "Mr. Shelmont says you torchbearing mutineers will never break down his castle doors. Dig that, if you can."

"What now?" Gilson whispered.

Luke thought about it, realizing that Shelmont had no idea what was going on. He thought his own guards were revolting. That was a laugh. What a pathetic little man this superachiever must be. Yet he knew exactly what Shelmont would want to hear right now; the mad tyrants of history gave good example. He whispered instructions to Gilson.

Gilson shrugged and rolled his eyes but repeated what he was told. "Tell Mr. Shelmont that I, his last loyal servant, choose to die by his side in defense of his glorious ideals."

"Huh?"

"Tell him that. Word for word."

"Up to you. Hold on."

They waited. Five seconds later the door slid open.

They walked down a steel corridor brightly lit by fluorescents. The secretary's desk was at the end. She saw Luke, and her eyes widened. Luke touched the barrel of his revolver to his lips, indicating silence. She nodded.

"Open that one," Luke said, cocking his jaw toward the next door.

"But that's Mr. Shelmont's private area. And you have to wear paper aprons. He'll fire me!"

Luke aimed his gun at her. "So will I."

She gulped. She pressed a button on her desk.

The door slid open with a faint pneumatic squeak.

Jonathan Shelmont stood there in a red smoking jacket with his arms thrown wide open, his face twisted in an ugly mixture of fear and gladness.

"Comrade Gilson," he cried, but then his eyes snapped over to Luke, snapped over to his hand that held the .357 Magnum. The faint trace of color in his pale face vanished in an instant.

"Traitors!" he shrieked, backing away.

There was a Uzi on his desk. He went for it.

Luke popped off a shot over his head. The noise thundered in the steel enclosure like cannon fire. Shelmont skidded on his shoeless feet and fell to his knees. He began to sneeze.

Luke stalked over to him. "Where's Larry Vandevere?"

Shelmont sniffed. "Go to hell!"

Luke kicked him squarely in his pale face.

Shelmont sprawled over backward and slid to the wall. A bright trickle of blood dripped out of his nose. "Stop!" he shouted, shielding his face. "In the basement! In the basement!"

Luke hauled him to his feet and planted his pistol barrel against his forehead. "Show me."

Blubbering and sneezing, Shelmont let himself be pushed forward. As they passed through the outer door, leaving Gilson and the stunned secretary behind, he stopped suddenly and turned.

"I'll pay you," he said. "More money than you've ever imagined. Fifty thousand dollars, maybe more. The cops don't pay you that much, do they? What are you, SWAT or something? I'll pay you one hundred thousand dollars to let me go."

Luke smirked at him. "Get going."

"One hundred and fifty thousand. My final offer."

Luke rapped him over the head with the .357. "Move, asshole."

"Ow!"

They went downstairs, through more hallways and rooms to a kitchen that seemed to Luke to be large enough to put most restaurant kitchens to shame. At the east end of it was a simple wooden door. Shelmont stopped there.

"Two hundred thousand, friend. Set you up for life."

"Open it."

Shelmont opened it. Now Luke could hear a strange, rhythmic whacking sound below, the sound of someone methodically beating something. Following each whack, he heard a low, animal groan. He frowned, filled with a sudden premonition.

"Let's go," he said.

They went down. The first basement room was dark. Tall shadows of boxes and crates bulked to the ceiling. There was a faint dank odor in the air, the smell of fresh blood. Light spilled out of an adjoining room. Luke took a handful of Shelmont's hair and tugged him along behind himself. He came to the open doorway and stood in the light, looking in.

A huge bear of a man was busy pounding something with a bloody length of garden hose.

His back was to Luke; the thing on the floor twitched and flopped each time it was hit. Luke saw bare feet. The toenails had been ripped out. A bleeding hand, also without nails, reached up in spastic fashion to ward off a blow; the big man slapped it casually aside.

Luke's insides went icy cold; he tried to speak and found that his voice had frozen in his throat.

Shelmont sneezed.

The big man turned. Sweat glistened on his long, mournful face in the harsh light cast by a single bulb.

As he turned, Luke could clearly see Larry Vandevere's head resting on the bloody cement floor, a misshapen lump of flesh. His mouth hung open like a corpse's. Only one shattered bit of tooth was visible there. Tufts of his hair had been pulled out, probably with pliers, and the naked scalp had bled. There were black cigarette burns on his cheeks and swollen eyelids.

Numb with horror, Luke raised his hand to bring his pistol to bear squarely on the big man's forehead.

"Five hundred thousand," Shelmont said. "Listen to reason."

Luke blew a dime-sized hole between Manning's eyes.

Blood and brains blew out the back of his head to splatter on the cinder-block wall. He crumpled to the floor, dead, his eyes open. The bloody hose rolled out of his opening hand.

Luke jerked Shelmont into the room, shaking with outrage. He picked up the hose and hauled back with it. Shelmont squealed and covered his face, cringing against the wall. "One million dollars," he squeaked. "Cash money."

"Pick him up," Luke said. "Pick him up or I swear I'll beat you to death."

Sneezing, Shelmont bent down over Larry. "I'll get blood all over me," he complained. "This jacket's silk, you know."

Luke hit him with the hose, cracking it across his back with a satisfying thump.

Shelmont screamed and waltzed around the room clawing at his back. "Ow! Jesus! *Achoo*! Shit! Ow, ow, ow!"

"Pick him up," Luke growled.

"All right, all right." Shelmont bent down and disdainfully hoisted Larry up into his arms. He straightened with a groan. "Now what?"

"Where's the CIA man?"

"Who?"

Luke hit him again. Shelmont whooped, spinning in circles. "In Tahiti!" he shrieked. "He accepted a bribe!"

"Okay. Outside."

"Allow me to offer you two million. My final offer."

Thump! Shelmont screamed and spun in circles with Larry dangling limply in his arms. When he had recovered, they went into the next room, up the stairs, through the kitchen and maze of hallways and rooms to the ruined front door. Shelmont was breathing hard by then. He stepped over the dead guard, moaning.

"Christ, my fucking door. Do you know how much that cost me?"

Luke thumped him hard across the back of the neck. While he pranced and screamed, Luke recovered his M203 and loaded the launcher with an incendiary grenade. Whining, Shelmont went outside with Luke sticking close behind him.

The sound of Tran's battle still raged distantly in the east. Gilson and the young secretary were by the gate, trying unsuccessfully to climb over. At the guardhouse Luke pulled the dead man out and found the switch that opened the gate.

"Okay, walk," he told Shelmont.

"Three million," Shelmont panted. "My final offer."

Luke turned and lobbed the grenade through the front door. It burst in a dazzling shower of white phosphorus particles, igniting every combustible object it touched. In seconds the carpet and wallpaper were on fire.

"My God," Shelmont said. "Not that."

Luke hit him again, then once more just for the good feeling of it before he discarded the rubber hose. Shelmont screamed and cursed and made more final offers. He had reached six million by the time they came to the golf cart Luke had abandoned.

"Cash," he gasped, sitting inside with Larry still in his arms. "More money than a peasant like you ever dreamed of."

"I've already got six million," Luke said. He swung out with the .357 and hit him in the mouth. Once again Shelmont screamed, and this time when he was done, he was spitting out teeth.

"That's for calling me a peasant," Luke informed him.

They drove east. "Talk to me, Frags," Luke said into his mike as they came within sighting distance of the guard barracks. In the moonlight he could see the small figure of Tran Cao scuttling back and forth on the roof.

Tran sounded irritated and out of breath when he replied, "How long I gotta keep this up, Luke? Two times now I almost fall off. Plus they shoot through the roof and make me dancing."

"My, your English gets bad under stress," Luke said. "I'm heading for the eastern shore now. Time to disengage and report to your pickup site."

"Finally. Can you divert these guys while I climb down a drainpipe? We're all getting very tired of this."

"Sure thing. Drop an incendiary down the chimney before you go, will you?"

"Okay. Just give me some elbow room."

Luke swung toward the barracks. Staying out of range of the Uzis, he began hurling grenades as he drove. Bright explosions lit the night. Soon a few searchlights began trailing toward him, followed by bobbing flashlights. He saw Tran's dark figure disappear over the lip of the roof.

"Now your nightmare has come true," Luke said to Shelmont. "Your own men are after you."

"Seven million," Shelmont replied wearily. "My final offer."

They came to the shore, a mild escarpment of jagged white stones. Luke urged Shelmont out, and together they

made their way across the rocks to the water's edge. Luke
slipped his night-vision goggles on and scanned the water.
Moonlight danced on it in heaving pinpoints of green.

No boat.

No Ben.

"Can I put this guy down?" Shelmont asked.

"Do it and you die," Luke responded. He rummaged
through his bag and counted eighteen 40-mm HE grenades, two incendiaries, and five standard fragmentation
grenades. Enough, maybe, to hold the guards off for a few
minutes. He loaded one into his launcher, turned, and fired
it toward the oncoming lights. It landed short.

A dozen Uzis responded. Bullets plunked into the water
and sparked off the stones.

Shelmont dropped down with a yelp of fear and a
sneeze. Luke went down on his stomach and began lob-
bing HE grenades in earnest, laying down a semicircular
field of fire.

When a cart veered close he used his .357 and shot the
driver in the face. The cart careened on, bounced down the
escarpment, and slammed upside-down into the water with
a tremendous splash.

For hired guards Luke had to tip his hat to some of
them; they were intensely dedicated. In other circumstances
Luke would be pleased to hire some of them. Perhaps that
day would arrive if he didn't have to kill them all first.

He fired a grenade point-blank into an oncoming cart,
blowing it into pieces that wheeled and flapped through the
air. In the brilliant flash he could see seven or eight men
low-crawling toward the shore. With sincere regret he
loaded an incendiary into the launcher and lobbed it
toward them. He hastily removed his goggles before it
burst.

When it did, screams of horror filled the night.

Four men jumped to their feet with their pizza suits

roaring into sudden flame. They jittered and danced, running in aimless circles as incandescent white phosphorus particles sank through their skin to eat at the bone.

One charged past Luke into the water, a screaming human torch. Luke ended his agony with a single pistol shot.

The others eventually fell over and quit screaming. Their Uzis burped as the flame exploded the cartridges in their magazines.

The survivors charged on regardless, firing steadily, dark, stalking figures in the flickering firelight. The stench of burned hair and flesh wafted on the breeze. Shelmont, terrified, buried his face against Larry's stomach and screamed.

"Tell them to back off," Luke shouted, and reached over to shake him.

Shelmont raised his face. It was smeared with Larry's blood. In the dancing light his eyes were wild and wet. He sneezed.

"Tell them!"

"Men!" Shelmont screamed. "It's me! Mr. Shelmont! Don't shoot!"

It had no effect. Luke was not surprised. The guards were too deep in the heat of battle, no longer fighting for Shelmont but for themselves. Friends had died tonight. They would not stop until victory or defeat ended the battle.

"I order you," Shelmont shouted, rising to his knees, and as Luke reached to haul him back down, he heard the familiar *thup* of a bullet striking flesh.

Shelmont wobbled on his knees. He clasped his hands to his throat and turned to Luke with wide and mystified eyes. He opened his mouth as if to speak.

Blood founted out of his mouth in a large red splash. He chewed it, grimacing. His chest heaved.

He dropped his hands and Luke saw the hole in his throat.

Shelmont's face contorted. For a second Luke thought he was going to cry, but then he emitted a thundering sneeze that blew out of the hole in his throat with a noise like a tremendous wet fart, spraying blood and mucus, tearing it wide open.

He dropped unceremoniously forward on his face.

Luke fired more grenades, growing quietly desperate. There were three 40-mms left in the bag, the five fragmentations, and one incendiary. He began to toss grenades overhand, maintaining his field of fire but realizing that it was irrevocably shrinking.

He threw the last grenade and went back to the 40-mms.

That's when he heard the approaching sound of a powerboat.

It had to be Ben. *Had* to be.

He backed into the water, dragging Larry and his M203. When it was chest-deep he inflated his flotation vest and drifted out.

Bullets spatted into the water all around them. One sizzled past his ear, making it hum.

With difficulty he loaded the last incendiary and fired it at the shore, creating a wall of fire. The water at the shore bubbled and hissed.

The boat drew closer. An M16 barked. Two M16s barked.

And then it was beside them, and hands were reaching down to haul them aboard.

Epilogue

"Crap," Jake O'Bannion said six days later as he came up the stairs onto the redwood deck.

Luke didn't look up from the newspaper he was reading. He had been so absorbed in the unfolding story of corruption and scandal—this was a day-old Chicago paper in his hands—that he hadn't heard the buzz of the gyrocopter as Jake returned from his trip to Higgery and the post office. A brilliant sun shone down on the Arizona desert, and a gentle breeze rustled the edges of the paper. There had been another leisurely late-morning breakfast here in the heart of the Superstition Mountains.

"Here," Jake grunted. He plopped down in a chair and handed him two envelopes. "Ever notice that nobody ever writes to me? Not even my ex-wives."

"Lucky for you," Luke said. He studied the envelopes, seeming lost in concentration.

"Well?" Jake said after a moment.

"Well, what?"

"Aren't you going to open them? One's from Missy."

"I know that. I am attempting a psychic reading."

Jake's jaw dropped. "Don't tell me you can do that too."

"The mind of man has incredible powers."

Jake nodded. "The body too. When me and Calvin and Missy picked you guys out of that boat on the beach, I thought Vandevere was dead. Deader than shit. He got blood all over the van we rented. And that was tough on Missy, seeing her dad like that."

"She took it well enough. And the paper says he's been upgraded from critical to serious, so he'll pull through. He'll be whole again just in time for the grand jury."

"Do I have to be psychic to predict that heads are going to roll?"

"Hundreds of heads, Jake. This Shelmont affair is turning the entire Chicago bureaucracy on its ear."

"Think they'll ever find out who fought the war on Shelmont's island? I'd hate to see you go to jail."

"I doubt it. Even if they suspected DFI, the CIA would cover our asses. Remember, we were technically in their employ. If you think Shelmont was good at applying pressure, wait till you see what the Agency can do if it has to."

"Good for them, I guess."

He stared wistfully at the envelopes, fidgeting. "Well?"

Luke narrowed his eyes. "Missy says thank you for saving her dad. *Thank you* appears seventeen times in the letter. She says the nurse she is staying with while her dad heals up doesn't know what to do with all the money I gave her. The nurse said that for this kind of money, Missy can stay all year. Missy is glad to be away from that stuffy private school her dad makes her go to. She also says her daddy looks funny when he smiles because he has no front teeth left. She wants to know how we are going to get her dad's car back to him. She says thank you again, and ends the letter."

Jake leaned forward. "Okay, prove it."

"Any bets on this one?"

"A case of Jack Daniel's, and the loser has to drive Larry's car to Chicago. If you're psychic, I'm Polish. And you know I'm not Polish."

"Fine." Luke opened the letter and read it silently, nodding at times. Then he wadded it up.

"I win."

"No fair," Jake cried.

"Care to try it yourself? This letter's from Cal Steeples."

"Damn right I'll try it." Jake took the envelope and touched a corner of it to his forehead. He frowned and grimaced.

"Cal says thanks so much for the huge paycheck. He says he worried himself sick about the IRS for no reason. The IRS took one look at his files and gave up in disgust, decided his flight business was small change, anyway, and left him alone. Further, he states that his girlfriend and him finally ate a duck, whatever that means. *Thank you* appears one time in the letter."

Luke grinned. "Case of Jack and a trip to Chicago? Notwithstanding the fact that Cal probably told you this would happen while you were on the way to pick us up after you rented the van at Midway Airport?"

"Case of Jack and a trip to Chicago."

Jake opened the letter and read it. He nodded and wadded it up. "I win."

"I guess we're even," Luke said. "We'll both drive to Chicago and take turns getting drunk on the way."

And a week later that is exactly what they did.